Shadows of Light

Season 1 Episode 1
From the Shadows

To Dawn + Rick

Aaron Torrence

Aaron Torrence

ISBN 978-1-63844-228-8 (paperback)
ISBN 978-1-63844-229-5 (digital)

Christian Faith Publishing
832 Park Avenue
Meadville, PA 16335
www.christianfaithpublishing.com

Printed in the United States of America

Prologue

Ever since the kingdom of Luminous was first founded, it has been under the protection and guidance of the three Guardians chosen by the Light.

Originally, when the Light first created everything, the world had no darkness. Humans introduced it into the world after breaking a promise with the Light. Out of concern for his people, the Light allowed himself to be consumed by darkness for three days. When he returned, he brought with him the sun, moon, and stars as a sign that humanity would no longer have to live in total darkness. He then tied the life-force of these celestial bodies to three individuals he chose himself and told them to take care of the people until he returned to destroy darkness entirely. These three individuals became the three Guardians and were gifted with special powers to help them in the tasks that were given to them.

The first Guardian is the Prophet, who holds the power of the stars. The Prophet's job is to teach the people. They let the people know what is right and what is wrong as well as tell them what the Light's will is. In order to accomplish this, they have been gifted with the ability to dream of future events. These dreams are given to the Prophet by the Light himself and will always come to pass.

The next Guardian is the Warrior, who holds the power of the moon. Their job is to protect the people. They patrol the streets in the dead of night and stop anyone who tries to hurt or threaten another. To give them an edge in battle, they have been gifted with the ability to fuse with any shadow. With this power, not even total darkness can keep evil from being found out.

The last Guardian, but certainly not the least, is the Ruler, who holds the power of the sun. Their job is to lead the people. They are to make laws and pass judgments that support order and righteousness, and they also take steps to help their people survive during difficult times. As a symbol of their authority, they have been gifted with the ability to control natural light. Through their own light, they are meant to remind others of *the* Light.

Whenever one of these Guardians died or became unable to do their job, the Light simply chose a new Guardian to take their place. Thus, the kingdom of Luminous has always had the three Guardians.

At least, it used to.

When the most recent Ruler died, everyone waited for the Light to choose a new Ruler. However, for some unknown reason, the Light remained silent. No Ruler was chosen; and without a Ruler, the sun itself stopped rising, keeping Luminous plunged in an eternal night.

One year passed and no sign of the sun or the new Ruler. It was at this point that a scientist named Saul Leos led an uprising that ended with him becoming the first Ruler *not* chosen by the Light. With his newfound authority, Saul led the kingdom in a new direction, one that tried to abandon the Light and make humanity more self-sufficient. With this goal in mind, Saul and his underlings began to develop new technologies that sought to match the powers of the Light and the three Guardians.

Not everyone was happy with this change though. A small number of people still loyal to the old regime formed a rebellion called Shadows of Light, or S.o.L. for short. Using a combination of espionage and guerilla tactics, they try to cripple Saul's army with the ultimate goal of overthrowing him.

Nine years have passed since the previous Ruler died. Many people, even those in S.o.L., have lost hope that the Light will ever choose a new Ruler, but the war between S.o.L. and Saul's empire continues.

Chapter 1

The concert was completely sold out. The largest outdoor auditorium in all of Luminous was now standing-room only. Only one singer/songwriter could have attracted a crowd this large, and that was Sarah Leos. Two years prior, she made a strong first impression with her hit single, "Light up Like the Sun," and she has since risen to the top of the charts. Now at eighteen years old, she was planning her biggest concert ever in celebration of her father's eight-year anniversary as king of Luminous.

The crowd cheered as Sarah walked onstage. She was wearing tight jeans, a white long-sleeve shirt, and a gold-colored vest. Her long blond hair flowed freely behind her, and her blue eyes were complemented by a large friendly smile. She gave the crowd an energetic wave hello. As soon as the crowd's cheers died down, she took a microphone from its stand and said, "Hello, everyone! Are we ready to have fun tonight?"

The crowd cheered once again, and Sarah continued. "Today we celebrate a momentous occasion! Eight years ago, on this day, humanity chose a Ruler for us when the Light would not. In those eight years, he has brought many technical marvels that allowed us to survive this Long Night. You know him as our honorable king, but I know him as something better—my dad, Saul Leos!"

More cheers were heard from the crowd; but unbeknownst to both the crowd and Sarah, there were other people present who were not as happy about her speech. Hiding on the roof of the auditorium were four shadows—or at least four people dressed like shadows. All of them were dressed head-to-toe in black: shoes, pants, utility belts, long-sleeve shirts, breastplate, gloves, and, to top it all off, a facemask covering the lower half of their faces.

The first of these four had short black hair, dark-blue eyes, a light skin tone, and had a small war-hammer on his belt. The second was the only girl of the group with shoulder-length black hair and similar features to the previous person; she was carrying around a pair of knuckles. The third had a light skin tone, smooth brown hair, brown eyes that were nervously looking around, and had a medium-sized rectangular shield for a weapon. The last of these mysterious figures had dark skin, spiky black hair, and was armed with a pair of tonfa.

"Here we are, guys," the one with the shield whispered. "Our first mission. You guys remember the plan?"

"Heck yeah," the hammer-wielding one whispered back. "When Saul comes onstage to make his guest appearance, we short out the lights with an EMP, lower ourselves down to the stage with our grapple lines, then grab him and hightail it to the woods before anyone even realizes what happened! Can't wait to put it to action!"

"Just remember," the shield-user added. "We have to be quick. Just the minimum amount of bounding and gagging. We can tie him up better once we're safe in the forest."

"Yeah, yeah," the knuckle-wielding girl said. "We practiced this a million times back in headquarters. We know what we're doing."

"Sorry. Just a bit nervous."

The one with the tonfa spoke up. "We all are, but we need to control ourselves and focus on the task at hand. We were trusted with this important of a mission as our first one. We have a chance to make a strong first impression and possibly end Saul's reign for good! We can't allow nerves to distract us."

"Speaking of distractions," the girl said. "I think Sarah's finishing her speech. Get ready, everyone."

"Seven years of training all coming to this," the tonfa-user said softly, more to himself than anything.

The four peeked over the edge of the roof as Sarah continued her speech. "Given the occasion, I really wanted to have my dad come onstage and say a few words to all of you! Unfortunately, he was simply too busy and had to cancel last minute! However, he was at least able to create a video for you! Please pay attention to the screen behind me and enjoy!"

The aforementioned screen turned on and showed a man in his late forties with dull blond hair and a thin band of gold encircling his head. This was Saul Leos, the current king of Luminous. "Good evening, everyone," the recording of Saul said. "Sorry I couldn't be there in person. I just wanted to say that I'm flattered that my daughter would go through all this trouble for me, and I am proud of what she has done during her career."

As the video of Saul continued to play, the four people in black stared in disbelief at what they just heard.

"What?" the hammer-wielder whispered. "The fake king isn't even here?"

The knuckle-wielding girl spoke up. "We can't proceed with the kidnapping mission if the target is a no-show," then turning to the one with the shield, "What do we do, Agent Pitch?"

"I-I don't know," Pitch, the shield-user, said. "Watcher said we *needed* to do this mission. I'm at a complete loss."

At this point, Saul's speech had ended, and Sarah started her first song, a recent one of hers titled "Make Our Own Light." Her voice sang out loudly and beautifully.

Many years ago, the sun just died
And by now we're sure that it won't rise.
But in this Long Night we still thrive.
We don't need the Light to survive!

We will make our own light!
We will fight our own fights!
We will reach the highest heights!
We will make our own light!

As the crowd cheered that first chorus, the four shadows on the roof sneered in disgust.

"Let's just go," the hammer guy suggested. "A failed mission is better than listening to this propaganda."

"For once, I actually agree with you, Bat," Pitch said. Then to the knuckle-wielding girl. "Moth, your thoughts?"

"Same. No real reason to stay here," Moth replied.

Pitch nodded and turned to the guy with the tonfa, but before he could say anything, a PEW! sound was heard, and a white laser struck between two of them, barely missing! They turned around and saw their assailant. They instantly recognized the distinctive armor of Saul's army. The soldier was dressed all in white, wearing a thick breastplate with a glowing blue battery right in the center. Wires ran across his arms, connecting to a disk attached to the palms of his gauntlets, from which he had fired the laser. Finally, the soldier wore a helmet and visor that completely covered the upper half of his face. The soldier brought a finger to the side of his helmet and shouted, "Intruders spotted! S.o.L. agents confirmed. Move to the roof immediately!"

Before anyone could say anything else, Bat began rushing toward the soldier! He pressed a button on his hammer, and certain panels began glowing blue with electricity! One POW! BZZZT! was enough to bring the soldier down, twitching with paralysis! But it was too late, and more soldiers began climbing onto the roof shooting lasers! The other agents in black activated their own weapons and prepared for a fight!

The crowd below, understandably, flew into a panic upon hearing the laser blasts and were already running toward the exit in droves. Screams soon became louder than the lasers. Sarah, meanwhile, looked around in shock of what was happening. Unsure what else to do, she yelled in her microphone as loud as she could, "Everyone! This is an emergency! Make your way to the nearest exit immediately!"

She wasn't sure if anyone could hear her over the lasers and the screaming, but it was really all that she could do. She took a wary step backward and watched the audience to make sure everyone got away safely.

Up on the roof, the agents were doing their best to fight off the waves of soldiers. Bat and Moth were the main attackers of the four, running up and hitting the soldiers with their hammer and knuckles with reckless abandon! Pitch watched their backs by tossing bolas at some of the more problematic-looking soldiers, all while using his shield to deal with those who got too close to him personally! Finally, the last agent was using his tonfa to pick off any soldiers left behind with deadly precision!

However, during a moment where he was near the edge of the roof, a stray laser blasted the rubble underneath him, causing him to fall to the stage below! As he fell, he dropped his tonfa and shielded his head with his arms! He landed with a THUD! on his side before rolling onto his front with a groan!

The fall startled Sarah and caused her to fall onto her rear with a "Yeek!" She stared in shock as this random guy with spiky black hair picked himself up. It took her a while to register that the guy was wearing a S.o.L. uniform. When she realized that, she turned around and tried to crawl away, hoping that he wouldn't notice her.

But as she was crawling, she heard something just as concerning—a sharp CRACK! sound amid the lasers. She looked above her and found that the structure which supported the overhead stage lights had been riddled with stray laser fire, and it looked like a rather large chunk was dangling precariously right above her. With the worst possible luck, another laser blasted that critical juncture, causing it to fall! Sarah tried to dive out of the way, but she was just a moment too slow, and the structure landed with a sickening CRUNCH! on her left leg. She let out a painful "AAAHHHHH!"

The agent who fell had just recovered his tonfa and was going to contact his teammates when he heard the scream. He looked over and saw Sarah trapped underneath the debris. He looked up at the roof, where his team was still fighting, then back to Sarah then back to the roof again. Finally, he made up his mind and ran toward Sarah.

Sarah was just shy of panicking when someone touched her shoulder. She looked up and saw it was the agent, causing her to cross the line and freak out. She tried to crawl away, but her leg was still trapped, and struggling only made it hurt worse! Then a calm, soothing voice spoke to her. "Calm down," the agent said. "Look at me."

Doing her best to stifle her fears, she looked at the agent, who had pulled down his facemask to let her see his whole face. He was about her age, with dark-colored skin and deep grey eyes that were piercing yet oddly soothing. He had a calm, sympathetic expression that made one feel like everything was going to be fine. He spoke again, stressing every syllable to make sure she understood. "I am not going to hurt you," he said. "You are going to be okay. Trust me."

Sarah inexplicably found herself willing to believe this grey-eyed agent. With her tears starting to dry, she slowly nodded to show she understood. The agent brought his mask back up and went to try and lift the debris off her leg. Unfortunately, he was interrupted by a laser blast!

One of the soldiers had come onstage and was now taking shots toward the agent, either not noticing or not caring about Sarah's presence! With the lasers now just barely missing her, Sarah panicked and cried out, "Stop shooting! Please!"

The soldier did not listen and just kept shooting lasers! Sarah screamed and covered her head with her arms. The agent simply gave a small "ugh" in frustration and knelt in front of Sarah to shield her! But just as he braced himself for a laser, a cable dropped down from the ceiling; and sliding down that cable was the female agent, Moth! She landed behind the soldier and gave him a few electrified jabs with her knuckles, stunning and bringing him down!

The male agent got back on his feet with a sigh of relief. "Thanks for the save," he said. "There's an injured civilian here. Do you mind helping me free her?"

Moth looked and saw that it was Sarah who was trapped. She took that in for a moment before going, "Um, okay, I guess."

"Good," the male agent said. "I'll lift the debris. You pull her away."

Sarah watched as this new female agent grabbed her arm. Honestly, she was still in a daze, so she made no attempts at struggling. The male agent lifted the debris off Sarah's leg with a groan.

With that, Moth pulled Sarah a few feet forward to safety. Once that was done, she let go of Sarah, who then slowly flipped herself over so that she was no longer on her stomach. The grey-eyed agent dropped the debris and went over to Sarah. "Listen," he told her. "I need to examine your leg. It might hurt a little, so be prepared."

Sarah nodded, and the grey-eyed agent began poking her left leg in various places. Each poke brought a different exclamation of pain from Sarah. "Thought so—broken," the grey-eyed agent said, then turning to Moth, "How's the fight going on up there?"

"Excellently!" Moth replied. "The herd of soldiers has thinned out, and while I wish I could bust a few more heads, we finally have a chance for a clean getaway."

"Good," the grey-eyed agent said. "You all go ahead and escape without me. I'll carry this girl to safety. I'll meet you at the rendezvous point."

"Are you sure?"

"Yes, I'm sure. Now go before more soldiers arrive."

Moth saw there was no point arguing, so she used the line she let down earlier to climb back up to the roof and rejoin Pitch and Bat. The grey-eyed agent, meanwhile, slung Sarah's left arm over his shoulder and helped her to stand up on her right leg.

"Do you have a vehicle nearby?" he asked her.

"I-I came here by helicopter," Sarah replied. "It should still be behind the auditorium."

"Perfect," the agent said. "Let's just take this slow and steady."

The agent slowly led Sarah off the stage and around the auditorium, making sure that she wasn't putting pressure on her broken leg. They were halfway around the building when Sarah gained the composure to speak up. "C-can I ask you a question?" she asked.

"Depends on what it is," the agent replied.

With that, Sarah asked the question that was plaguing her mind for the past few minutes. "Why did you save me?" she asked. "I'm the daughter of your organization's worst enemy. I write songs that go against everything you guys stand for. So, why even consider helping me out?"

"Don't get the wrong idea," the agent said. "I want nothing more than to see your father taken down, and since you support his ideals, I'm not a fan of you or your songs either. However, while you might be Saul's daughter, you are also a non-combatant. You never should've been a part of this battle, and I'm sorry you got injured during it. To put it simply, I just couldn't stand by and do nothing."

Sarah let that sink as they reached the back of the auditorium which had a field behind it; and in the center of that field was a large white-and-gold luxury helicopter with Sarah's name painted on the side. Members of Sarah's team were in and around the aircraft as well as a few soldiers acting as guards. As soon as they saw a S.o.L. agent approaching, they instantly raised their gauntlets.

"Hold your fire!" the agent shouted. "This girl is injured! You need to take her to safety!"

Unlike the one onstage, these soldiers did lower their weapons, albeit with much reluctance and a lot of begging from the team members. The agent carried Sarah the last few feet to the helicopter and handed her off to one of the team members.

"Her left leg is broken. Take her to a hospital immediately."

"Okay, we will," the member said, sounding relieved that Sarah was alive.

With that, the agent simply gave a nod and ran off. The soldiers tried to take one last potshot at him, but they were too late, and he made it to the safety of the forest surrounding them. Once he was gone, the manager of the team cried out, "Everyone in the helicopter! We are taking Sarah to the hospital!"

Everyone got in and closed the helicopter doors. The helicopter then took off and was heading toward their destination. Sarah was made to lie on a lounge chair to keep pressure off her leg. She didn't mind. In fact, she was strangely quiet during this whole thing. The team knew Sarah as a very cheerful girl who was always willing to converse with her team, so it was weird for them to see her this quiet.

"Sarah?" the manager said. "You okay?"

This startled Sarah out of her thoughts and almost made her jump from her seat. "Oh! Sorry. I was a bit distracted," she said.

"Yeah, I'm okay—I mean apart from the broken leg, but other than that, I'm okay."

Her team was sure that she must have a lot on her mind after the events of that night, so they just left her alone after that. The truth, however, was exactly the opposite. As Sarah returned to her thoughts, for some reason not fully known to her, all she could think about was that grey-eyed agent who saved her life.

CHAPTER 2

The grey-eyed agent of S.o.L. thanked the Light he managed to make it to the woods. The woods just outside Luminous was actually one of the few areas a S.o.L. agent could travel safely due to the lack of artificial light, making their black uniforms almost invisible. As long as they kept their heads and didn't stray too far from the edge of the city, they usually weren't in danger of getting lost. With this in mind, the grey-eyed agent kept a close eye out for his team's chosen rendezvous point: an alleyway with WHEN WILL THIS NIGHT END?! graffitied with red paint on the side of one of the buildings.

The agent finally found that alleyway and was relieved to find that Pitch, Bat, and Moth had already arrived safely. Moth was leaning against the wall with her arms crossed in front of her. Right beside her was Bat, who, without his mask, could clearly be seen as Moth's twin brother. Finally, Pitch was pacing back and forth with some worry on his face. Bat was the first to notice the arrival of their fourth member. "There you are, Justin!" he said, calling the agent by name. "Took you long enough!"

Justin rushed forward and placed a hand over Bat's mouth. "Quiet!" He warned him. "We might be finished with our mission, but we're not out of danger yet. Stick to code names until we reach the safety of HQ."

Bat pushed Justin's arm away. "Whatever," he said. "I am *not* calling you Agent 327. Seriously, when are you gonna choose a *real* codename?"

"Whenever I come up with a good one," Justin replied. "But since I haven't yet, it's 327 or nothing."

Pitch spoke up at this point. "Well, codename or no codename, we're glad you're safe," he said. "Now come on. Let's get back to HQ."

"Good idea," Justin said. "Let's hurry and get the inevitable chewing-out over with."

Moth spoke, "A chewing-out for what?"

"A failed mission, an unnecessary battle, an injured civilian," Justin counted off. "All things considered, this whole event was an absolute disaster, so yes, I'm expecting for the higher-ups to be mad."

Bat voiced his opinion on the matter. "But none of those things are our fault," he said.

"I KNOW THAT!" Justin exclaimed.

Everyone went silent for a moment as they saw the pain in Justin's eyes.

"I know that," Justin repeated. "But our fault or not, Saul's empire is going to use this event to make us look like the aggressors. Most people already have a low opinion of us; and this whole battle, at a *concert* for *civilians*, is just going to make our public perception worse. Maybe it would've been better if we never accepted this mission in the first place."

Everyone stayed silent. As much as they hated to admit it, they actually agreed with Justin to some degree. Eventually, Pitch sighed and said, "Let's just go." He then placed a finger over his earpiece and said, "Agent Pitch to base. We have successfully rendezvoused with 327. Heading back to HQ now."

With that, the S.o.L. agents let down the fire escape and climbed onto the roof. Apart from the forest, the rooftops were S.o.L. agents' other most used means of getting around the city. It helped them avoid being seen by the people below, and the buildings were usually close enough together that they weren't in danger of missing a jump. After a few seconds of traveling over the rooftops, Moth decided to break the silence. "So, 327?" she said. "You get a kiss from that girl you rescued?"

"No. And there are several reasons why that is a stupid question," Justin replied. "First, romance is too big a distraction to even consider during a war. It just causes unnecessary amounts of worry especially over whether you'll ever see each other again—as if we don't deal with that enough. Second, even if I were to consider the risk of romance…you do realize the girl I saved was Sarah Leos, the daughter of our worst enemy? The girl who cheerfully sings songs that go against everything we stand for? Why would that girl kiss me or vice versa?"

"I was just teasing you, sheesh," Moth replied. "Thought it would lighten the mood."

"Maybe next time, try a knock-knock joke instead," Justin dryly responded.

"Okay, I admit, good comeback," Moth replied.

"You want to embarrass someone, Moth?" Pitch joined with a mischievous look in his eyes. "Why don't you tell 327 about the results of your competition with Bat?"

"Don't…you…dare," Moth said venomously.

"Twenty-two to eighteen, my favor!" Bat said with no reservations. "Making me the first who-can-beat-the-most-soldiers champion!"

"Just wait till next time, twin brother," Moth said. "I'll crush you then."

"Keep telling yourself that, sister," Bat replied.

The gang hopped across a few more roofs and arrived at the roof of a four-story legal firm. The most notable feature of this rooftop was the door that led to the building's stairway. This stairway was the entrance to S.o.L.'s secret headquarters. Justin and the others entered in and climbed all the way down to the basement—a basement that none of the normal employees or visitors even considered visiting. The agents pushed open the door and entered a massive underground complex with S.o.L. agents wandering around everywhere. Justin and the others let out a massive sigh of relief that they were finally home.

Two people were already waiting for them. One was a grey-haired woman with world-weary eyes and light-colored skin. This was Martha Capris, codename Nocturne, second-in-command of S.o.L. and the one who kept track of individual agents and what they were doing. Standing right beside her, however, was S.o.L.'s de facto leader—a middle-aged man with dark-colored skin, a military buzzcut that just started getting some grey, and a black long coat over his S.o.L. uniform. Before the Long Night started, he was known as General Cyrus Ares; now, he only went by Director Dusk.

"Welcome back, agents," Dusk greeted them.

"Good to be back, sir," Pitch said. "Though I wish it could've been in more successful circumstances."

Martha spoke up, "We heard over the news. It seems your team's first mission did not go so well, did it, Daniel?"

Pitch, now answering to his real name, replied, "No it did not. Most of it was out of our control, but there are still some things we could've done differently that might've helped."

"Well, we look forward to hearing the full story during the debriefing," Martha said. "How is everyone feeling, by the way?"

"Xavier, Molly, and I managed to avoid serious injury," Daniel said, using Bat and Moth's real names. "However, I suggest Justin visit the infirmary for an examination."

"Why?" Justin spoke up. "You can see I'm clearly fine."

"*You fell off a building*," Daniel pointed out. "There is no way you didn't receive *some* injury from that."

"I'm fine," Justin insisted, only to be met by Daniel's unconvinced stare. "Okay, so my right side might still be a *little* sore, but it's nothing I can't handle."

"I'm sorry, Justin," Martha said. "But you should take Daniel's advice and visit the infirmary. That's an order."

Justin sighed. "Yes, ma'am."

"Sorry, Justin," Daniel said. "I know how you feel, but we need to make sure you're okay. No taking unnecessary risks."

Director Dusk spoke up again. "With that settled, we will be expecting all of you in the conference room at 2200 hours for the debriefing. That gives you over an hour to rest up, get a medical examination, and think about the events of your mission. Any objections?"

Hearing none, the agents were dismissed. Molly and Xavier went to their respective rooms to rest up. Daniel went to the storeroom to try and restock on bolas that he couldn't recover during battle. Justin, meanwhile, reluctantly headed over to the infirmary.

Justin honestly didn't have anything against the infirmary itself, nor did he mind the lead doctor, Amelia Centaurus, codename Doc. However, he knew that if she found even the smallest injury on him, she would force him to sit out on any future missions until he fully recovered, and Justin did not want to sit out on any opportunity to cripple Saul's empire. Maybe it was workaholism. Maybe it was pure obsession, but Justin had spent the past seven years training to become an agent of S.o.L., and it just didn't seem right to him to take a break after only one mission.

Justin went into the infirmary and found that he actually wasn't the only patient there. Sitting on one of the patient beds was a man in his early seventies with thick silvery-grey hair and a moderate number of wrinkles. He had a warm smile and surprisingly bright eyes for someone his age. This was Blake Sagittaire, S.o.L.'s chief engineer.

"Justin! You're back! Good to see you!" he said. "How was your mission?"

"Hey, Blake," Justin said, unable to hold back a small grin upon seeing the old man. "The mission was a failure."

A look of surprise crossed Blake's face. "Really?" he asked.

"Really," Justin replied. "A soldier spotted us, leading to a large-scale battle that caused mass panic and injured one civilian. The worst part is Saul didn't even show up to the concert! So even if we never got caught, the mission would've been a failure anyway!"

"Saul didn't show up?" Blake repeated. "Are you sure?"

"They replaced his live speech with a prerecorded one," Justin told him. "Apparently, he canceled last minute."

Blake sorrowfully looked at the palm of his right hand. There, glowing a bright white, was a pattern of three stars. "I guess I misunderstood that particular vision," he said.

Blake, in addition to being chief engineer, was also the Light's chosen Prophet. The insignia on his right hand marked him and served as proof that he had been chosen to wield the power of the stars. Whenever he slept, he was figuratively watching out for any sign of a vision from the Light, which is how he got his codename—Watcher. The visions of the future he received had helped many of S.o.L.'s most important missions; but for some reason, not this one. "It seemed so promising a vision too," Blake said wistfully. "Saul had agreed to make an appearance at the concert. I then saw the four of you getting into position. Then my eyes were drawn away to the distance where the sun finally rose again! I thought it was a sign that this mission would be key to ending this war."

"If only it were that easy," Justin lamented.

Blake took a deep breath and slowly let it out. "Oh well," he said, regaining some of his cheerfulness. "It's not the first time I've been wrong about a vision. The visions that the Prophet receives will always come true, but it's not always clear how they will come true. I'm sure we'll understand what this vision means in time."

"Sure," Justin said unconvincingly. "By the way, why are you here in the infirmary?"

"Just a simple checkup," Blake said. "At my age, it's a good idea to make sure my health stays in good condition."

At this point, a female voice spoke up. "In that case, you'll be glad to know your blood test results are in and everything looks good."

Doctor Centaurus returned from the back of the infirmary. She was in her late thirties with small narrow eyes and long straight black hair. She wore a lab coat in addition to the standard S.o.L. uniform and carried a tablet in her hand. "Everything from cholesterol levels to iron is at much healthier levels that they were one year ago," she continued. "It seems taking on an apprentice has helped you out considerably."

"She has lightened my workload and made sure I'm not missing any meals," Blake admitted. "But sometimes..."

As if on cue, the door to the infirmary burst open, and a girl with tan skin and long brown hair rushed in. She was around Justin's age, with an almost manic look in her eyes. "Mr. Sagittaire! Mr. Sagittaire! I did it!" she shouted.

Blake cleaned out his ears and gave a good-natured sigh. "Hannah, I know you're excited," he said. "But couldn't you wait until after I returned to the lab?"

Hannah Aquare, codename Candle, rubbed the back of her head in embarrassment. "Sorry," she said. "I just finished my new invention and really wanted your thoughts on it."

"Very well," Blake said. "What is it?"

"This!" Hannah said, producing a remote-like contraption from her belt. "This handy doodad sends a signal that can crack open electronic locks from up to twenty feet away! No stealing passcodes or cracking encryption. Just point and *ding*!—Saul's whole security is practically rendered useless!"

"Until they start using old-fashioned lock and key," Justin snarked.

"Hey! This thing can make infiltration missions ten times easier for agents. Don't knock it," Hannah said. "Let me show you. Dr. Centaurus, do you mind if I lock the infirmary for a minute?"

"I'd rather you not," Dr. Centaurus replied. "Just in case someone has an emergency and needs to enter."

"*Please!*" Hannah begged. "Just for a minute."

"Ugh. Fine," the doctor said. "Do it quickly."

"Thank you!" Hannah exclaimed.

She immediately went over to the panel next to the door and pushed a button. The green light at the top right corner of the panel turned red to show the door was locked. "All right!" Hannah said. "Now watch. All you got to do is point and…"

She pressed a button on her device. Everyone waited, but nothing happened. The red light stayed red. Hannah pressed the button a few more times—still to no avail. "Ugh. This worked in the lab," she insisted.

She pressed the button one more time and held it, but instead of unlocking the door, the end of the device burst into flames! "Aah!" Hannah screamed as she dropped the device and began stomping on the flames, putting them out!

Hannah looked sadly at the broken remains of her device as Dr. Centaurus unlocked the door manually. "I swear it was working in the lab…" Hannah insisted.

"I believe you," Blake said, placing a comforting hand on her shoulder. "But you have to remember invention is a process. Prototypes don't always do what you want them to, and it sometimes takes hundreds of tries before a device works properly. Let's go back to the lab, and I'll help you with it—that is, if Dr. Centaurus doesn't need me for anything else?"

"No. You're free to go," the doctor said. "Just remember to take your vitamin D supplements. I swear, nine years with no sunlight, and people are *still* forgetting to take them."

Justin sighed. "I guess it's my turn now," he said. "I was really hoping this distraction would last a little longer."

"And what exactly are you here for, Mr. Libra?" the doctor asked Justin.

"My team is just being cautious," Justin said. "I fell off a building during our mission and…"

"YOU FELL OFF A BUILDING?!" everyone shouted.

"I'm fine!" Justin insisted. "It was the backstage to the auditorium. It was barely one story. Nothing to worry about."

"I'll be the judge of that," the doctor said. "To the x-ray. Now!"

Justin rolled his eyes and headed to the back of the infirmary where the x-ray was located. He lay down on the table, and the doctor activated the x-ray. Once the pictures were taken, she examined them closely. "The good news is you have no serious injury," she told him. "No broken bones or anything like that. Let me examine your side."

Not even waiting for permission, the doctor began poking Justin's body in various places. Justin tried to remain stoic, but he couldn't help but grunt in pain whenever she poked his right side. "There's definitely something wrong there," the doctor said. "Let me see it."

Justin took off his breastplate and raised his shirt slightly. Sure enough, an ugly purple bruise covered his right side. "I thought so," the doctor said. "Not much we can do other than wait for it to heal.

Bruised ribs usually take 1 month to heal fully, so I'm prescribing two weeks of rest followed by another two weeks of low-risk recon missions only."

"I'm fine!" Justin insisted. "I can continue going on missions."

Dr. Centaurus said nothing and instead poked Justin in the side again. The grunt of pain that followed showed that Justin was *not* fine. "That area is already damaged enough as is. You're lucky that you don't have any major fractures. We don't want to risk damaging that area any more, and even if we were to take the risk, can you honestly say that the pain you're feeling won't distract you during missions?" the doc told him. "I'm not taking any chances. Two weeks rest, two weeks recon only, and if you don't cooperate, I will let Martha and Director Dusk know."

Justin knew he wasn't going to win this battle, so with some frustration, he pulled down his shirt, put his breastplate back on, and said, "Fine."

"If the pain gets too bad, you can always put some ice on it," the doctor said. "Come back here after your two weeks of rest for a follow-up. I need to make sure it's actually healing before you do any missions. Got that?"

"Got it," Justin replied.

"Good. You are free to go," the doctor said.

Justin wordlessly got up and began to leave, passing Blake and Hannah, who had stayed to make sure he was okay.

"Justin, do you want to talk?" Blake offered.

Justin took a deep breath. "Thanks, Blake, but I'll get over it," Justin said. "I think I just need some fresh air to calm myself. I'll be on the roof if you need anything."

Justin left the infirmary and went to the roof. He sat down near the edge, looking toward the forest and outer edge of the city. It was more relaxing than looking deeper into the city, which only caused him to think about how much control Saul had over it. Right now, though, he just tried to relax and get used to the idea of not going on any big missions for the next month.

Suddenly, he heard a male voice behind him. "How're you enjoying the view, Justin?"

Standing behind Justin was a man in his midthirties. He was tall, with light-colored skin, spiky brown hair, and a warm, friendly smile. In addition to the usual S.o.L. uniform, he was wearing a long black scarf which billowed heroically in the breeze. This was S.o.L.'s top agent and the Light's chosen Warrior, John Percy, codename Lunar.

"Blake told me what happened," John said, taking a seat next to Justin. "How're you handling things?"

Justin gave a sigh. "I'd be lying if I said I wasn't a little frustrated. I've been training for seven years to become an agent, and after just one mission, I'm forced to sit on the sidelines for a month—all because of a bruised rib."

"Don't let it get you down, Justin," John replied. "In a dangerous business such as this, injuries are to be expected. All agents have to deal with them from time to time."

"You don't," Justin responded. "You're the Warrior! Whenever you're about to get injured, all you have to do is turn to shadow to avoid it entirely."

"My powers can help me avoid harm, yes," John admitted, taking off his right glove to look at the blue waxing moon insignia glowing on his palm. "But they are not an end-all be-all solution. There have been times where I either couldn't activate my powers or just didn't do it in time and ended up getting injured as a result. Believe me, I know exactly how you are feeling. Not being able to do anything is a big pile of raven droppings, but you have to look after yourself as well as others."

"Maybe," Justin said. "I'm still annoyed though. It's just some pain in my side. I can still help my team. Sometimes you have to take a risk if you know you can help, right?"

"Sometimes," John said. "But I don't think this is one of those times. Your team is more than capable of covering for you while you rest, and if they ever do need help, literally every single agent here would be willing to step in. You don't have to do everything yourself, so maybe slow down and consider all your other options before taking any risks."

Justin remained silent as he took that all in. “If it helps,” John said, “I could talk to Dusk and see if I can join you on your first recon mission when you recover.”

“Really?” Justin asked, confused. “You, our top agent, join me on a simple recon mission?”

“Hey, training new agents is part of my job,” John pointed out. “I’m already slated to be going on plenty of missions with the rest of your teammates over the next few weeks. You don’t want them to have all the fun, do you? So what do you say?”

Justin needed only a few seconds to consider. “Yeah, that sounds cool.”

“Alright,” John said, giving Justin a fist bump. “I’m heading out on my nightly patrol of the city. You prepare for your mission debriefing and then get some rest. See you.”

With that, John literally vanished before Justin’s eyes. It looked as if he had turned to smoke, though really it was just him fusing with the shadows of the night. Justin had to wonder what it felt like to just become a literal shadow, but he figured he could ask John that question another time.

Justin took one last breath of fresh air and went back inside headquarters. He had a debriefing to attend, followed by what was sure to be two weeks of boredom, but at least he now had something to look forward to once that was done. What could go wrong?

CHAPTER 3

The door to Sarah's hospital room flew open as Saul rushed inside to visit his daughter. It had been a couple hours since the attack at the concert, and Sarah was currently resting in bed, her left leg in a cast and suspended. A guard was hired to not let anyone in until "morning" to ensure that she got some rest. However, as her father *and* the king, Saul was the exception. "Sarah!" he cried out with worry. "I came as soon as I could. Are you okay?"

"Hi, Dad!" she said, giving him the best one-handed hug she could without moving too much. "I'm fine. The doctors say I will recover though obviously it's gonna be a few months."

"Well that's a relief," Saul replied. "Just let me know who did this to you, and I'll make sure every single soldier in Luminous is out looking for them."

"Nobody did this to me, Dad," Sarah told him. "A piece of rubble broke off, and I was unlucky enough to be under it. I appreciate the sentiment though."

"Hmm," Saul said. "In that case, maybe I should build an anti-gravity device and get revenge on the laws of physics instead."

Both Sarah and Saul had a small chuckle at that. However, Saul's features immediately hardened afterward. "Curse the Light for letting this happen!" Saul said. "If *I* had known this would happen, I…"

"But you didn't know, so stop worrying about it," Sarah reminded him. "Things could have turned out a lot worse, all things considered."

"True," Saul admitted. "So, you give any thought about how you're gonna make up for this concert?"

"Well, I would *like* to have a follow-up concert once I've fully recovered," Sarah mentioned. "But given how long that will take, I'm not sure how feasible that is. I'll talk with my manager tomorrow. Most likely we'll give everyone a portion of their ticket price back as an apology, maybe throw in a free CD or something. I don't know. I write music. I sing it. I let others handle the rest."

Saul gave a small chuckle at that. "Yeah, I can imagine that other stuff is not nearly as fun," he admitted. "Whatever your team does, though, I suggest that your next concert be given better security."

"Oh, I'm sure that's gonna be number 1 priority," Sarah assured her father.

"That's good," Saul said. "I realize there's probably going to be a lot on your mind over the next few months, so if you want to talk to me about anything, just ask."

"Well," Sarah said hesitantly. There was certainly something on her mind that was bugging her, but she wasn't sure if she should tell her dad about it.

Saul noticed her hesitation. "Is something wrong?" he asked.

Sarah stayed quiet for a moment longer, gathering her thoughts. She decided that if she couldn't share her thoughts with her dad, who could she share them with? "Honestly, something happened during the concert that I'm having a hard time wrapping my head around."

"Well, what is it?" Saul asked.

Sarah took a deep breath. "When my leg was trapped underneath that rubble, it was a S.o.L. agent who saved me," she told him.

"Really?" Saul said with a raised eyebrow.

"Yes," Sarah said. "He even knew who I was too. I thought that S.o.L. agents were ruthless extremists, but this agent risked his life to save someone he knew was on the opposite side, and I'm not sure what to think of that."

"Remember, Sarah," Saul told his daughter. "S.o.L. is all about giving people false hope. Hope that the Light has not abandoned us and that a new Ruler will be chosen eventually, and in this Long Night, I can easily imagine that some good people who are desperate to see sunlight again might choose to believe this lie instead of adapting to our new world. This agent you saw was probably one of those people. Who knows, maybe after some time, he'll realize the truth and quit S.o.L. in favor of our side."

"Maybe," Sarah said, not really looking at her father.

Saul gave a great big yawn. "Well, it's getting late," he said. "I better get out of here and let you rest. Do you need anything?"

"Hmm. Do you mind bringing me my guitar and computer next time you visit?" Sarah asked. "I might not be able to have any concerts while I'm recovering, but I should still be able to write new songs to share with my fans afterward. I don't want to go through this whole ordeal and not have something to give to them. They've already got it bad enough with how this concert turned out."

Saul gave a small smile and kissed Sarah on the forehead. "You've grown into a fine young woman," he said. "Here you are, your leg broken, and you still think of how to make other people happy. I'm proud of you. I just wish your mother could've seen who you've grown up to be."

Sarah actually never met her mother. Before she was born, her mother had caught a rare disease that the doctors couldn't cure. The best they could do was ensure Sarah didn't meet the same fate as her mother. "I wish so as well," Sarah told her father.

Saul took a deep breath to regain his composure. "Alright," he said. "I'll try to come again tomorrow. I'll bring your guitar and computer. Call me if you ever need anything else. Love you. Good night."

"Love you too, Dad," Sarah said. "Good night."

Saul left the hospital room with one last wave goodbye. With her father now gone, Sarah thought back to what he said about the S.o.L. agent who saved her. She desperately wanted to believe that agent was simply a victim of false hope; it was the only thing that made sense to her worldview. So, why did she hesitate?

Looking back, that grey-eyed agent didn't seem like the kind of person naïve enough to fall for a clear deception, nor did he seem desperate enough to follow one anyway. Then again, what did she know? She had only been with him a few minutes. Was that really enough time to get to know someone? Well, she knew that he was brave and kind and confident. Oh, what was she thinking? The point was he didn't *seem* like he was living a lie.

Basically, she was left with two options—either S.o.L. was as deceptive as she believed and she misinterpreted the grey-eyed agent's character entirely, or he, and by extension, S.o.L., was genuinely good and she was the one who was living a lie. Oh, how she wished there was a third option.

A large yawn interrupted her thoughts. She supposed it was getting late and she really should be getting some rest after what she went through. As she adjusted herself in her hospital bed, she decided that she could save those questions about the grey-eyed agent for another night.

CHAPTER 4

Two weeks after that failed mission at the concert, Justin's bruised rib had healed enough for Doctor Centaurus to clear him for reconnaissance missions—about time, in Justin's opinion. He had never really gotten into any leisure activities like reading or listening to music, and he was only allowed the bare minimum of physical training because of his injury, which caused the past two weeks to be unbearably boring for him. Only two things made it tolerable. The first was the conversations he had with the other S.o.L. members. Even if he personally couldn't do anything, he could always find John, Blake and Hannah, or his teammates and ask about what they did. The second was the knowledge that John would be joining him on his first mission upon recovery.

And now the time had finally come. Justin and John left HQ and began running on the rooftops toward the center of Luminous. According to the mission briefing, one of the empire's warehouses just received a large shipment of neo-plastic, an energy-resistant material that both parties used to make armor and weapons. S.o.L. wanted to send in agents to steal some of this neo-plastic; but before they did so, they needed Justin and John to scope out the area and figure out what kind of security to expect.

There were indeed a few patrols around the warehouse district though not as many as expected. There were about fifty warehouses in the area, but as Justin and John looked through binoculars on the nearest rooftop, they could only count roughly a half-dozen soldiers moving around. It was possible they missed some due to the size of the area they had to scan, but it still seemed like a small number. "Maybe they're all standing guard inside?" Justin theorized.

"Or everyone took their coffee break at the same time," John said sarcastically while also taking pictures with a miniature camera. "In all honesty, though, your theory is not too far-fetched. With something as valuable as neo-plastic, they probably don't want to let it out of their sight. But would they really sacrifice the security of everything else here? Surely there are other valuables stored in these buildings."

"I don't see any cameras either," Justin pointed out. "At least not any outside. Should we go in for a closer look?"

"Good idea, agent 327," John stated.

He then took out a phone-like device out of his belt and looked at the screen, which showed a map of the area. He then pointed to a certain warehouse a few rows to their right. "There's our destination," he told Justin. "Follow me. We need to approach quickly but cautiously. We approach from the back. You ready for some action?"

"You bet," Justin said with a smirk underneath his facemask.

The two agents climbed down from the roof. Unfortunately, the warehouses were spread too far apart for rooftop travel to be viable, so they had to risk the ground. They ran as quick as they could toward the designated warehouse. When they arrived, they cautiously moved along the side of the building until they could peek around the corner of the front. One lone soldier was standing guard in front of an open door with a dull orange light pouring out.

John pulled his head back and placed his hand on his chin in thought. Justin, however, upon seeing there was just one guard, activated his electric tonfa and rushed out! Justin dealt a few quick blows to the guard, knocking him out before he even had a chance to raise an alarm! He dragged the unconscious guard over to the side of the building, where John, in quiet exasperation, asked "*What* are you *doing*?"

"What did I do wrong?" Justin asked, mildly annoyed. "We need to get inside. This guy was guarding the only way in. I took him out as stealthily as possible. That's how we usually do things."

"On a normal mission, yes," John pointed out. "But this is a recon mission, and one of our goals is to make sure no one learns we were here. When this guy wakes up, he'll tell his superiors what happened, which will most likely lead to them increasing security, making it harder for our agents during the actual mission. We should weigh our options, see if there is any other possible courses of action before resorting to violence."

Thinking about it, Justin had to admit his actions did seem a little short-sighted. Swallowing his pride, he took a deep breath and said, "You're right. I'm sorry, Lunar."

"It's okay, 327," John replied. "In all honesty, I can't think of any sneakier way in, so we probably would've had to take out this guard anyway. We'll just have to tell our superiors what happened and let them know there will likely be more soldiers than we counted. Just remember, next time, make absolutely sure there are no other options first."

"Yes, sir," Justin said.

"Now, let's check what's inside this place," John said.

They sneaked around to the front, and John peered inside the warehouse. He then walked inside with Justin following him. Inside, dozens of large crates and palettes of neo-plastic were spread across the warehouse, front to back. From the high ceiling, old-fashioned lights cast an orange glow over everything; but most importantly, there was no sign of guards or cameras anywhere.

"This seems too easy," Justin said.

"I know," John agreed. "That's what worries me most. Saul's empire is misguided, but they're not idiots."

John and Justin took another quick look-around, even more cautious than before. John looked back toward the entrance and paused. "327," he said. "Look at the floor in front of the entrance."

Justin looked and noticed that a long thin gap in the floor was placed right inside the entrance. He kneeled down to look inside and found a metal sheet that seemed like it could reach the ceiling if it was let out of that gap. "What is this?" Justin asked.

"I have an idea," John stated. "Do you notice anything…*wrong* about this warehouse, 327?"

"Um, aside from this gap and the lack of security, not really," Justin said. "Why? Do you notice something?"

"Come outside for a sec," John said, heading out the door.

Justin followed, and John pointed him toward the side of the building. "Look how long this warehouse is," John said, with Justin obeying. "Now look inside."

Justin looked back inside and saw what John was talking about. The back wall was *way* closer than what the outside said it should be. "Th-the inside is too small," Justin said, confused.

"Exactly," John said, heading back inside. "So either the architect was a madman, or something is not right here."

John and Justin headed toward the back wall to examine it. Upon closer inspection, the wall was sticking out of a gap similar to the one that was at the front of the warehouse. With this knowledge, they inspected the wall further until one portion pushed inward slightly. The two agents pushed this hidden door open slightly further to reveal another room behind the wall. This room, however, they dared not enter.

Unlike the empty front, the back was crawling with soldiers and scientists checking computers that lined the walls. Cameras were also seen in the corners of the roof. However, all that paled in comparison to the centerpiece of the room. A tower of white platforms stacked on top of each other almost reaching the ceiling. Four of those platforms were connected to a laser turret manned by a soldier, each one spread far enough apart to not interrupt the other. The soldiers spun the turrets 360-degrees around the tower while simultaneously adjusting the angle of the turrets themselves, showing potentially no blind spots in its aim.

"That does not look good," Justin said, stating the obvious.

"It's worse than that," John said. "That tower of cannons has the potential to be the ultimate anti-S.o.L. weapon. The height takes advantage of our lack of ranged weapons, and for the few we do have, their effectiveness is lessened by the multiple cannons. If one cannoneer gets incapacitated, the others can cover for him until they recover. And if Saul's empire has learned anything about our tactics, I'm willing to bet they made it immune to EMP waves as well. This is all a trap."

"A trap?" Justin asked.

"The neo-plastic is meant solely to bring us here," John explained. "The lack of guards and cameras is meant to lull us into a false sense of security. Then when we enter this warehouse, that wall at the entrance is raised, trapping us in. When that happens, this wall is lowered, putting us in the firing line of that tower. There are just two things I haven't figured out yet. First, how are they going to know when we enter the warehouse without any guards or cameras? Second, how are we going to deal with that tower? If the lights were off, I could simply shadow-fuse to reach each cannoneer in quick succession, but I don't see a light switch, meaning they must be computer-controlled, and the ceiling is too high for any of our EMP weapons to reach. Even if I could turn out the lights, how would a normal agent handle this?"

One of the scientists brought a ladder over to the tower, allowing the soldier at the top to climb down. "Works good so far," the soldier said. "Kinda wish I could actually fire this beauty though."

"We need to keep things quiet just in case any S.o.L. agents are scouting outside," the scientist reminded him. "Don't worry though. We performed a thorough weapons test at the castle's lab before bringing the turrets here. They should work perfectly fine when S.o.L. comes sneaking around."

"Sick," the soldier said with a grin. "So how long do I have to destroy those agents before this needs a recharge?"

The scientist chuckled softly. "You needn't worry about that," he said. "The Turret Tower is connected directly to this warehouse's main powerline. As long as this warehouse has power, it can practically go on forever. However, if a power outage were to occur, the tower also has an emergency battery that will last for one hour, so in that situation you will need to take out those S.o.L. pests quickly."

That information caught John's attention. "Well, well," he said, taking out his mini-binoculars. "Let's see if we can make use of that info."

John was silent for a few seconds as he searched the room. "Yes! This place still has a fuse box on the back wall," he said, then, "Raven droppings! It's locked. Passcode protected."

"Is there any way to figure out the passcode?" Justin asked.

"Not as far as I can tell," John replied. "It's too risky to enter the room and search through paperwork, and I highly doubt anyone is planning to input that password anytime soon. I say we should return to base and let everyone know about our findings. If they do decide to proceed with this mission, they're just going to have to infiltrate the power plant as well and cut off power from there though that comes with its own problems. Personally, I hope they decide this neo-plastic is just not worth it."

Justin had to agree. If the Light's chosen Warrior was nervous about fighting a piece of tech, Justin did not want anyone else going up against it.

The two agents took a few pictures and quietly closed the secret door before quickly going back outside. However, upon exiting the warehouse, a bright light suddenly shone on their right, blindsiding them!

"Freeze!" a harsh voice called out. "You're under arrest for trespassing and high treason!"

The agents' eyes adjusted to the light, and they got a good look at their situation. A line of soldiers blocked the path to their left. On their right were a few more soldiers but, more importantly, a large military all-terrain vehicle with a giant search light attached to the back pointing right at the agents. A figure standing beside the search light stepped forward to reveal himself fully. He was wearing a modified version of the white soldier uniform with no helmet and green highlights on the gloves and chest plate. He looked to be in his upper forties with dirty blond hair in a military buzzcut, two dark-green eyes, and a smirk that only came with a love of inflicting pain. Attached to his belt were two large metal gauntlets with mysterious attachments. John recognized this figure.

"General Scorpius," he said. "I should've known. This whole thing has your twisted mind written all over it."

Justin could barely believe what he just heard. "Wait," he said. "General *Scorpius*? You don't mean…"

"Yes," John replied. "*The* General Ryan Scorpius, aka the Assassin—Saul's second-in-command and one of his Four Horsemen Generals."

In general, Justin tried to keep a calm demeanor. However, upon hearing the identity of who they were facing, Justin began to feel the icy hand of dread crawl up his spine. Justin had heard stories of the Assassin; and if even half of them were true, he knew he had every reason to fear for his life.

CHAPTER 5

When Saul first rose to power, he chose four of his closest allies to lead his army as his generals. Each one was also a skilled scientist in their own right and used their talents to give themselves unique weapons more powerful than anything that came before them. The deadly potential of these weapons was so great that they were given the apocalyptic title of the Four Horsemen Generals; and of the Four Horsemen Generals, Ryan Scorpius, AKA the Assassin, was considered the most cunning and the most deadly.

And now that same general had trapped Justin and John between two squads of soldiers.

Justin's mind raced as he wondered how they were going to get out of this situation. John, however, seemed to keep some level of calm.

"How'd you even know we were here, Scorpius?" he asked almost nonchalantly. "There were no cameras and no guards who spotted us as far as I recall."

Scorpius chuckled softly to himself, the light from the search light beside him just making him look more menacing. "It's quite simple really," he said. "The soldier who was guarding this warehouse had a new sensor planted in his armor. If it senses a strong electric current, like the kind your weapons generate, it sends a signal straight to the main security room located elsewhere on the premises. We knew you were here the moment you knocked out that soldier and entered the warehouse. A near-perfect anti-S.o.L. warning system, don't you think so, Warrior?"

"Impressive, I admit," John said. "But it won't do you much good. We already know about the Turret Tower, and we're taking that information back to our allies so they can avoid this entire trap."

"Ah, yes, the Turret Tower," Scorpius said reminiscently. "It's too bad you couldn't have come by tomorrow when its weapon systems will be reactivated. If you did, we would've just sprung the trap and let our new toy take care of you. Oh well, we'll just save it for the next group of S.o.L. agents. It just means I get the pleasure of killing you myself."

"Don't bet on it," John said, sneakily loosening a pocket on his utility belt. Then in one quick motion, John drew a four-star shuriken and threw it at the search light! The shuriken in question had a glass dome in the center filled with a blue energy, which was released in the form of an EMP wave upon striking the lightbulb, disabling both it and the vehicle it was attached to! Taking advantage of the surprise move, he turned to Justin. "I'll distract the Assassin!" he said. "You find a way past those soldiers and *get out of here! Now!*"

Justin instinctively obeyed and rushed at the soldiers on their left while John took out a pair of combat batons and rushed toward Scorpius. A few soldiers blocked his path, allowing Scorpius to put on his special gauntlets and give a few more words to his troops. "Don't let anyone escape!" Scorpius called out. "Fight to the last man!"

Justin and his tonfa were hard at work, trying to take out the soldiers in his way. Justin's main strategy was to rush in and deliver a few quick but precise strikes, which was made slightly harder by the fact that the soldiers, having long-range weapons, kept trying to put as much distance between him and them as possible, leading to him having to dodge the occasional laser blast. That and the sheer number of soldiers made dealing with them tricky. So while he was slowly but surely taking out his foes one-by-one, he was still a ways away from making a clean getaway.

John, meanwhile, was demonstrating why he was S.o.L.'s best agent. He wasn't even using his shadow powers, but he was still taking out soldiers before they even had a chance to put distance between them! Thus, he completely incapacitated all the soldiers on his end in almost no time, which just left General Scorpius.

Scorpius activated his gauntlets, revealing the strange attachments on them to be retractable blades, four on each hand. The edges of each one of those blades were replaced with a green laser capable of cutting through almost anything. With a war cry, he leaped toward John, ready to slash!

John avoided the strike by turning to shadow! He re-emerged only to have Scorpius block his blow! The general followed with a swipe that John jumped backward to avoid! John rushed back, but his attacks were knocked aside! He turned to shadow just in time to avoid Scorpius's counter-attack! This continued on with neither side gaining the upper hand!

Justin took out another guard before dodging another laser blast! Taking out a small squad of soldiers was not easy especially with a bruised rib that was starting to ache again from all the physical activity! However, he only had three more guards to take out, then he could escape without any lasers tailing him! Seeing his goal so close was enough motivation for him to make the final push!

Meanwhile, John landed a kick straight into Scorpius's chest, knocking the general down! John went to deliver the final paralyzing blow, but Scorpius rolled out of the way!

Scorpius got up, looking slightly out of breath. "Okay," he said. "Time to get serious."

Scorpius pressed a button on his belt, activating a piece of tech that trumped even his clawed gauntlets. In a few seconds, the belt produced a wavy energy field that covered the general head to foot. The energy field shimmered before disappearing entirely, taking the general with it. Scorpius had become completely invisible.

John, however, did not seem impressed. "You've done this trick before, Scorpius!" he called out. "Or did you forget that I don't rely on colors to see when I'm in shadow form and can still track you easily!"

With that, John went into shadow form to pursue his adversary.

Things became quiet as Justin took out the last guard. He didn't notice, however, as he was too busy catching his breath. Just as he was ready to make a run to safety, John's voice suddenly cried out from behind him. "Look out!"

John had come out of his shadow form and tackled seemingly thin air mere inches away from Justin! The surprise of the encounter caused Justin to stumble and fall on his rear as he watched John roll on the ground, grappling with his invisible enemy! John then appeared to be knocked away, most likely by a kick! John got back up and tried to get back in a fighting stance, but he was stopped.

Justin watched in horror as General Scorpius re-materialized, showing that his right-hand blades were planted firmly in John's stomach. Scorpius pulled out the blades with a sickening SHICK!, causing John to fall backward against the wall of the nearby warehouse.

With trembling hands, John took off his right-hand glove and held out the glowing moon insignia defiantly. "I…will not be… the last one," he said, his tone confident but his breathing getting weaker. "The Light will choose…a new Warrior to take my place… just as he will one day…choose a new Ruler. I don't care what you, Saul, or anyone else says…the Light has not abandoned us. I…still… believe…"

With that, John closed his eyes and let out one last breath. His right arm drooped down to his side, the once bright insignia fading away until it disappeared entirely. Tears began to well in Justin's eyes as he witnessed what he thought was impossible. John Percy, the Light's chosen Warrior and S.o.L.'s best agent, was dead.

Scorpius stood over his victim like an artist admiring his work. He let out a low sinister chuckle that soon turned into full-blown evil laughter. "Heh heh. Heh heh heh heh. Ah HA HA HA HA HA HA!"

Hearing that laughter caused Justin's anger to boil until he suddenly charged forward with an anguished war cry! However, the experienced general simply smacked him away, the back of his metal gauntlet hitting Justin in his right side! Justin grimaced as the pain surrounding his ribs increased back to how it felt after the concert. To make matters worse, soldier reinforcements had just arrived, surrounding Justin and leveling their laser gauntlets directly at him. Justin braced himself for the end when suddenly Scorpius spoke up.

"Hold your fire, men," he said. Scorpius stepped forward, a satisfied cocky grin on his face. "We'll take this one as a prisoner," he said. "I know fresh meat when I see it. We might be able to get some information out of him if we…'persuade' him."

Justin's side was screaming in pain, his whole body was shivering uncontrollably, and he felt like he could throw up any minute. However, he was able to gather enough energy to talk back to the general. "D-don't bet on it!" he said, his voice showing a strange mixture of anger and fear.

"Huh, funny," Scorpius replied. "That's exactly what John Percy said when this battle started, and look what happened to him. I'd say I'm pretty good at making bets. Knock him out, and take him to the castle dungeon."

With that, Justin felt a metallic blow to the back of his head. His head started ringing as he fell into unconsciousness. The last thing his blurry vision saw was the sadistic general laughing triumphantly.

CHAPTER 6

Breaking News! The Light's chosen Warrior, John Percy, is dead after a busted operation in the Warehouse District. John Percy was many things: public enemy number 1, a high-ranking member of the rebel group Shadows of Light, and an outspoken opponent of King Saul. However, not even his shadow powers, given to him by the Light who abandoned us, could protect him when he and a fellow S.o.L. agent were caught sneaking around the Warehouse District by a group of soldiers led by General Scorpius, leading member of Saul's Four Horsemen Generals. No details have been released about why the S.o.L. agents were there or how the fight went, but it ended with John Percy paying for his rebellion with his life. The other S.o.L. agent, whose identity has not yet been released, was arrested and taken to the castle dungeon for questioning. More details as they develop.

That was the news broadcast that aired to all of Luminous. Anyone who was asleep at the time would surely hear it repeated in the daytime hours. The members of S.o.L., however, caught it as soon as it aired. They always had at least one agent keep an eye on the news since it often brought useful information about the aftermath of missions as well as upcoming events they might need to sabotage even if all that information was buried in propaganda. Daniel was the agent chosen for news surveillance that night, and when he heard the first sentence of that announcement, he immediately called Director Dusk, Martha, Blake, Hannah, Molly, and Xavier so they could see for themselves.

Everyone had the same reaction: silence—pure disbelieving silence. No one was sure what to say in response to losing two close friends and allies. Eventually, Molly was the first to speak up.

"W-we gotta do something!" she insisted. "We have to avenge John or save Justin or both! What can we do?"

Martha gave a large sigh as she hung her head. "I'm sorry, Molly," she said. "But I don't think there is anything we can do."

"Well, why not?!" Molly replied.

Xavier joined in. "Yeah, why not?!" he said, as eager for a fight as his sister.

Director Dusk took charge of the situation. "In regards to rescuing Justin, the castle dungeon is one of the most high-security places in all of Luminous, second only to Saul's Research Department and the Throne Room," he informed them. "All of our previous breakouts were only made possible thanks to John's powers. Sending normal agents in is suicide, and as you just saw, we no longer have John around to help us. And speaking of John, you talk of avenging him, but how exactly do you plan on doing that? Invading the castle? Fighting General Scorpius? We don't have the resources for either of those."

"But...but there must be *something* we can do!" Molly exclaimed.

"The only thing we can do is continue fighting for the cause they fought for," Director Dusk said. "Thank you for showing us this, Daniel. Martha, Blake, and I have some things to discuss. The rest of you are dismissed."

Daniel, Molly, Xavier, and Hannah saluted their superior and left the room. The three senior members of S.o.L. stood in silence for a while.

Eventually, Dusk spoke up. "Blake, don't take this the wrong way, but I just have to know."

"No. I did not have a vision about this," Blake replied, greatly disturbed. "First, my vision about the concert goes absolutely nowhere, and now I get no warning at all about John's death. Nothing has been going right, and I don't know why."

Martha then shared her thoughts. "I hate to even suggest this," she said. "But you don't suppose that the Light really has abandoned us, do you?"

"No! No!" Blake responded vehemently. "The Light must have *some* reason behind all this that we just don't know yet. He has to."

"I want to believe you, Blake," Martha said. "But I can't help but wonder. Now that John's dead...will the Warrior go the same way as the Ruler? Will we have to go without moonlight as well as sunlight?"

Dusk joined with an even matter-of-fact tone of voice. "Clouds have been blocking the sky all night. For the time being, we have no way of knowing whether the moon is still there or not."

"Then there's still hope for a new Warrior," Blake said.

"Maybe," Martha admitted. "But the Light hasn't chosen a new Ruler in nine years. Who are we to say it won't be the same with the Warrior?"

"The Light promised that humanity would never again be in total darkness," Blake said. "It's one of the reasons the three Guardians even exist. The Warrior and the Ruler have to come back someday."

Martha sighed. "I wish I had your optimism, Blake," she said. "But these past few years have not been kind to us."

Dusk then gave the final word. "Well, whether a new Warrior is chosen or not, we will still continue the fight against Saul," he said. "It will be harder, of course. We often relied on John's powers to accomplish otherwise impossible missions, but our other agents are still capable of dealing a blow to Saul's infrastructure. Our first priority should be to assign a new team to that warehouse reconnaissance mission."

"Sir, are you sure that's a good idea?" Martha asked. "We don't know what caused the mission to go wrong for John and Justin.

What if the next team we send makes the same mistake, and we end up losing more agents?"

"John was our best agent," Dusk reminded her. "He would've made sure that no serious mistakes were made during the mission. I feel confident in saying that the only reason the mission failed was because General Scorpius was too knowledgeable about John's usual tactics due to their previous encounters. But now that John's dead, the general is probably busy interrogating Justin or just patting himself on the back—meaning we need to get that recon info and steal that neo-plastic quickly *before* Scorpius returns and sets things back to high alert."

"Very well then, sir," Martha said.

"You can plan the operation without me," Blake said. "I need to lie down for a while."

"Go ahead," Dusk said. "We'll handle the rest from here."

Blake left the room, looking twice his already considerable age.

Martha then turned to Dusk. "So, what now?" she asked.

"First, we figure out how to break this news to the rest of our agents," Dusk replied. "Then we need to decide just who we will offer the recon mission to."

CHAPTER 7

Justin was currently sitting in the far corner of one of the castle dungeon's standard cells. It was a plain grey room with a barred window on the back wall looking outside. There were no lights in the room, and since the outside was always nighttime, Justin had barely enough light to see everything around him. A toilet sat along the back wall just a few feet away from the window. Along the side wall adjacent to Justin was a worn-out cot meant to serve as a sad excuse for a bed. Shackles attached to the wall were connected to Justin's wrists, preventing him from going too far away from the back wall.

Justin himself simply sulked quietly. He had no idea how long it had been since he was captured, but he guessed it was at least a few hours. His side was hurting less than when he was knocked out, but it still hurt more than it did before the mission. His utility belt and earpiece had also been taken away from him, so even if he could somehow break free of his shackles, he had no way to call for help and no weapons or gadgets to help him escape himself. There was really nothing he could do *other* than sulk.

The metal door of his cell suddenly slid open. Justin looked up to find General Scorpius stepping inside. "So, are you ready to talk?" he asked Justin, his trademark smirk on his face.

"I have a few choice words for you but nothing that will help you find out who I am or how to beat S.o.L.," Justin replied bitterly.

Scorpius chuckled softly. "Oh, we already know who you are, Justin Libra."

This information surprised Justin and almost made him lose his confidence. He tried to gather some of it back before asking, "How do you know?"

"We did a few identification tests while you were unconscious," Scorpius explained. "I admit we were surprised when no results came from the fingerprint or eye scan, but then we did the DNA test, always the most accurate, and discovered the reason why. You weren't in any of the other records because you were legally declared dead a little over seven years ago."

"Yeah, all because of Saul and the rest of you guys," Justin said, regaining some bitterness after being reminded of that time.

"And let me guess," Scorpius continued. "After what happened, you decided that you would then join the rebels and trained these past seven years to become a S.o.L. agent."

"Not quite," Justin said. "They were the ones who found me and offered to take me in—a far cry from how your guys treated me."

"You should've been honored," Scorpius said. "You were being taken to a reform institution that would've removed any rebellious ideas your mom and pop might've given you. But you had to be a crybaby and run away—all because your stupid parents were dead."

This struck a nerve with Justin. He got up and rushed toward Scorpius! However, his shackles stopped him before he could actually reach the general! As he growled and glared, Scorpius shook his head. "Tsk, tsk, tsk," he said, taking a remote out of his belt. "Such temper. I'm going to have to discipline you for that."

Scorpius pressed a button, and immediately, Justin felt an electric shock from his shackles. The pain didn't last long, but it was enough to make Justin fall to the ground with an "AUGH!"

"Let that be a lesson to you," Scorpius said. "Now, enough about you. How about you tell us where to find S.o.L.'s secret headquarters?"

Justin knew what would happen and braced himself for it. "No," he said.

As expected, Scorpius pressed the button, and Justin felt another electric shock. "A pity, but not unexpected," Scorpius said. "I guess you would need *some* degree of loyalty to stay with S.o.L. for seven years. So let's start small instead. Tell me, is this cell too dark for you?"

"Not really," Justin said. "The shadows help hide your ugly face."

"You know what," Scorpius said. "I'm so impressed by that comeback that I won't shock you for it. Nevertheless, here's the deal. You give me the identity of one S.o.L. agent—just one—and in return we will place a lamp in here to make your stay a little more comfortable. So go ahead, rat out that one person in S.o.L. you don't like. However, the more S.o.L. agents you tell us about, the more comforts we will add to your cell. Who knows, tell us enough and we might even consider freeing you. So, what do you say?"

"I say you can take your dinky little lamp and toss it in the trash!" Justin replied. "Because I'm not selling out even one of my fellow agents!"

Scorpius shrugged. "Very well then," he said. "You've only been here half a day. I guarantee that by the end of the week, you'll be begging to take me up on my offer. And you better give up on any hope of rescue or escape. The only person who's proven capable of breaking in or out of this place was John Percy, thanks to his powers. And in case you forgot, he's now dead."

Scorpius left the room, giving just one last shock as the door closed. Once Justin recovered, he picked himself up and returned to his corner. Now that he no longer had to keep a brave face in front of the general, he sat on the floor and wallowed in depression because Scorpius was right. The dungeon's security was infamous. The number of guards, the high-security locks on all the cell doors and other factors made escape seem impossible; and unlike S.o.L. agents before him, he could not wait and hope for John to come and break him out.

The worst part was he partially had himself to blame for it. He was the one who knocked out that guard with the planted sensor. Scorpius only knew they were at the warehouse because of that.

Maybe if he waited, he and John could've found a way inside the warehouse without taking out the guard, but his eagerness to fight Saul's men cost him his freedom and John his life.

His mind turned to the Light, that supernatural being said to know everything that would happen and always had a plan to bring his people through tough times. Admittedly, he was not as passionate a supporter of the Light as, say, Blake. In fact, he was one of the agents who had given up hope on a new Ruler being chosen. However, he still believed that humanity needed the Light to some degree and that the Light had not abandoned humanity entirely. Now, however, he had no idea what the Light was planning.

Then again, how could he know? He was just a young novice agent who failed his first two missions—broken, chained up, completely hopeless.

"Light, what do I do?" he asked, burying his head in his knees.

Then Justin felt a strange tingle in his right hand. Before Justin could ask what it was, an overwhelming sensation spread through his whole body! As Justin let out a grunt, he wondered if the shackles had been activated again, but this did not feel like an electric shock! It felt more like his body was disintegrating! When it was over, Justin keeled over onto his hands and knees, his eyes closed, his body feeling like it had been hollowed out.

When Justin opened his eyes, he was surprised to find that everything had changed. Everything was now a shadowy black. Not a featureless black—the window was a slightly lighter color than the rest of the room, and the shapes of everything were easier to see than they were before, but there was no color or texture. He looked at his own hands to find that they looked like an outline and nothing else—an outline which seemed to be missing something.

Justin looked on the floor beside him to find that his hands had somehow slipped out of his shackles! He immediately backed away from them as if they were a bomb and tried to rub his wrists in relief. However, when he tried, his hands simply passed through them! He panicked and tried patting the rest of his body only to find that his hands passed through it as well! He would have let out a few screams, but for some reason, no noise came out when he opened his mouth!

At this point, Justin was sure this was either a nightmare or some insanity-driven hallucination. Forget the fact that he had been there less than twenty-four hours; nothing he was experiencing made sense! He had to get out of there—but how?

The window—it was the only way. He pulled himself up to the window, intending to squeeze through the bars, but his new intangibility instead made him pass right through them. He got another surprise when he realized that the window he climbed out of was three stories above ground! Justin, sure that he would plummet, closed his eyes and braced for impact—but it never came. He opened his eyes to see that he had not fallen an inch and was just floating in the air.

This just freaked him out more. He almost backed right up inside the cell again, but he stopped himself and instead pushed himself off the walls and away from the castle! He had no idea what was happening and just kept flying forward out of instinct more than anything, but once the castle was far behind him, he began to wonder how he was going to get down.

Once he thought about going down, though, he actually started moving downward. When he realized what was happening, he panicked and only accelerated his descent! He braced himself for impact once more! This time, he did hit the ground, but strangely, it did not hurt. His three-story fall onto pavement felt more like he had fallen onto a pile of pillows.

Justin picked himself up and mindlessly began running forward. Ahead of him, to his newly-colorblind eyes, appeared to be a bright white area. He entered that area and was immediately overwhelmed! It stung like a million bandages were being ripped from his body at once, causing Justin to trip and fall over.

That small trip had hurt more than the three-story fall did. Justin grunted in pain, realizing a moment later that he was making sounds again. He opened his eyes, and to his relief, the world had returned to normal—colors and textures back where they should be. He gave his body an experimental touch and found it to be solid again. Looking around, he realized he was in one of Luminous's suburban outskirts and the white area he entered was light coming from a street lamp. Luckily, the street was empty at the moment; its residents either asleep or at some late-night gathering downtown. He had no idea how it happened, but Justin was now far away from the cells of the castle dungeon.

He brought his right hand up to his forehead to wipe away some sweat, but as he did so, he noticed something strange. There was a faint blue glow coming from underneath his glove. He removed his glove and stared wide-eyed at what he saw. On his palm was the waxing moon insignia of the Light's chosen Warrior.

Justin could say only one word: "What?"

CHAPTER 8

The office of General Scorpius was grey and empty; no plants or pictures to brighten things up, just a large desk covered in computer monitors, a high-backed swivel chair for the general, and a few less-comfortable metal chairs for guests. It was cold and efficient just like its owner.

Right now, Scorpius was in a video call with the lead scientist of the Turret Tower job. The scientist had a grin like a hyena and was eagerly rubbing his hands as if awaiting the chance to talk. Why deny him the opportunity?

"What's your status?" Scorpius inquired.

"Things couldn't be smoother if they were coated in butter, sir," the scientist said. "We just finished arming the Turret Tower. We are now fully operational."

"Excellent," Scorpius said with a grin. "Get the cannoneers into their turrets. Let them know the waiting game has begun. Evacuate everyone else from the building, and make sure all elements of the trap are set."

The scientist saluted and ended the call and the screen turned black. Scorpius turned to a different screen and put in the password for a special call line that led straight to Saul himself. The self-made monarch appeared onscreen, looking worn out but still dignified, sitting up straight.

"Ah, General Scorpius. Always good to hear from you," he said. "What do you need?"

"Just wanted to inform you that our trap in the warehouse district is now fully operational and ready for whenever those S.o.L. agents take a second try at that neo-plastic," Scorpius replied.

"Excellent," Saul said. "Although are you sure that S.o.L. will indeed try again? You did kill their best agent after all. They might decide to cut their losses and move on to a 'safer' job."

"Maybe," Scorpius said. "But remember—*I* killed their best agent, and currently, I am not in the warehouse district. This might give S.o.L. that little extra confidence needed to try again and fall right into our hands."

"I hope so," Saul responded. "We're using a pretty valuable material as bait. We cannot keep it in that warehouse forever. I'm going to give you three days. If S.o.L. doesn't show up within that time, we're going to have to scrap the project and send the neo-plastic to one of our weapons facilities."

"Thank you, your highness," Scorpius said. "Is there anything else I can do for you?"

"Just keep me updated on any further reports," Saul said. "Saul out."

The screen blipped to black, and Scorpius leaned back in his chair with his hands behind his head and a satisfied grin on his face. These past few days had turned out better than he could've hoped for. Instead of destroying just one group of S.o.L. agents with the Turret Tower, he had killed the Warrior, captured the agent that was with him, and now had a chance to trap a second group of agents. This had the potential to enforce a serious loss of morale in S.o.L.'s forces and bring them one step closer to total defeat. As long as nothing unexpected happened, everything should turn out perfectly.

At that point, the phone on his desk rang. It was the dungeon's personal hotline, so something must be happening in one of the cells. Maybe a prisoner was finally ready to talk, or maybe one simply died. One way to find out.

Scorpius picked up the phone. "General Scorpius speaking," he said.

A shaky timid voice was heard on the other end of the line. "Um, General, sir, this is George. I bring the prisoners their meals."

"Well, George, do you have anything to report?" Scorpius asked.

"Um, do you know the prisoner in cell 138?" George asked.

Cell 138, Justin's cell. "Yes, I know the prisoner," Scorpius replied. "I just finished my first interrogation with him not ten minutes ago. What about him?"

George's voice became even more stuttery, "W-well, sir, h-he's, um, *gone*, sir."

Scorpius slammed his fist on his desk and shouted, "WHAT DO YOU MEAN GONE?!"

"I-I don't know, sir! He's just gone!"

"There are fifty guards patrolling the dungeon hallways, over three hundred patrolling the castle grounds outside, all the cells are at least three stories aboveground with barred windows, the cell doors automatically lock when closed, and prisoners are chained to the wall at all times! Now tell me, how does a prisoner become 'gone' under those circumstances?!"

"I don't know, sir! I made sure it was the right cell, and I checked every corner. But he's not there! Two guards were with me. They'll back me up on this."

At this point, Scorpius had enough. "Just return to your post," he told George. "I'll look into this myself."

Scorpius angrily slammed the phone down and got up from his desk. He ran over to the cell that held Justin and took a look inside to verify the report was accurate. Sure enough, a pair of empty shackles lay on the floor, and Justin was nowhere to be seen.

Seething with anger, he went and found the nearest intercom. "Attention, everyone!" he screamed into the speaker. "We have a prisoner escape! Suspect is an eighteen-year old male, five-foot-nine, dark skin, and spiky black hair! Suspect was last seen in standard S.o.L. uniform minus the belt! Suspect was last seen unarmed but should still be considered dangerous! If you don't find him within ten minutes, begin searching the city! Try to capture him alive if possible, but lethal force is authorized! NOW MOVE OUT!"

Scorpius did not know how this prisoner had escaped, but he knew that Justin knew too much. If he managed to get back to S.o.L. headquarters, he would surely warn them about the Turret Tower, and Scorpius's perfectly laid trap would become useless, which was why Scorpius was going to try his best *not* to let that happen.

CHAPTER 9

Justin ran straight for downtown, away from the open empty streets of the suburbs, and toward the safety of alleyways and high rooftops. By the time he reached a dark empty alleyway, his side was aching and his breathing was heavy. Once he was sure he was safe, he took off his right-hand glove again. Sure enough, the moon insignia was still glowing brightly on his palm.

He pinched himself to make sure he wasn't dreaming. Nothing changed. He lifted his eyes up to the sky and asked, "What does this mean?"

The expected silence followed. Justin continued, "What have I done to be tasked with this? I'm a novice agent who has only gone on two failed missions. Why not choose one of S.o.L.'s top agents for a job as important as protecting the whole city? Why me?"

Justin watched the dark clouds drift slowly overhead. "There's no way I can do this," he continued. "You chose the wrong person. How am I supposed to live up to the reputation of John or any of the previous Warriors?! Dear Light, how will S.o.L. leadership react when they learn that a novice was chosen to replace their best agent? I can't do it."

He looked back down at his hand. The insignia adamantly stayed where it was. He gave a deep sigh and sat down on the ground, his back leaned against the wall. "I have so many questions," he said.

"And I don't know what to do. It's such a big responsibility, and it happened so suddenly."

He took a deep breath to try and calm himself and took one last look at his insignia. "Okay," he said. "I might not know why I was chosen, but it seems there's no getting out of it. So, let's calm down and think this through. The best person to tell is probably Watcher. He's the Prophet. It's his job to give advice and guidance. He should be able to help me break the news to the others and maybe figure out this whole Warrior thing in general. That sounds like a plan—get back to HQ and talk to Watcher, figure out where to go from there."

At that point, Justin heard footsteps coming his way. He got up, put his glove back on, and moved deeper into the alleyway. Sure enough, Imperial soldiers passed by him on the main road. "Of course, I actually need to get back to HQ first," Justin reminded himself.

He looked around, but the particular alleyway he was in did not seem to have any fire exits to climb up. Even if there were, he had a feeling the noise would surely attract the soldiers' attention. He figured the best thing to do would be to wait until they moved on and try to find another way to access the rooftops. He began to slowly back up.

KRUNCH!

He stepped on an empty drink can someone had littered! He watched as soldiers began entering the alleyway before turning and running as fast as he could! Behind him, he could hear someone say, "Target found! Get him!"

Justin turned a corner just as lasers started firing! He grabbed the lid off a passing trashcan and threw it at the soldier in front! It rebounded off the thick neo-plastic armor, barely doing anything more than provide a mild distraction! He turned another corner and ran for the main road! He felt lasers just barely miss him as he turned left and followed the road!

He knew he needed to find another alleyway to duck into before the soldiers caught up to him again! He saw one just ahead of him on his left and rushed toward it! Unfortunately, he couldn't shake his pursuers, and they saw him enter the alley! He needed to change strategies and fast!

He saw a fire escape just ahead of him! He thought if he couldn't lose the soldiers on the streets, he should try to lose them on the rooftops! He pulled down the ladder and climbed up as quick as he could! He pulled the ladder back up after him in the hopes it would delay his pursuers by at least a few seconds! He finally began ascending the fire escape as soldiers entered the alley and began shooting at him again! The metal stairs blocked most of the lasers, but Justin still experienced a few close calls!

Justin immediately took off as soon as he reached the rooftop! He jumped across to the nearest building and got a decent head start before feeling lasers nip at his heels again! He was a little concerned about the lack of cover on the rooftops, but he was still confident that the soldier's heavier armor would prevent them from making the same jumps he could.

He ran across a few more rooftops, barely dodging laser fire! Then a few roofs ahead of him, he saw, to his horror, more soldiers climbing onto the roofs! The other soldiers must have called for reinforcements! He needed to get off the roofs, or else he would be pinned! He looked at the side of the building he was currently on and, to his relief, found a fire escape! He began climbing down it to the alley below, soldiers still following him!

Justin ran through a few more alleyways before he ran into his worst nightmare—a dead end! He could still hear the footsteps of pursuing soldiers not too far away! For a moment, he thought this might be the end for him as he had no weapons and no means of escape!

Then he remembered—he was the Warrior now! He could just turn into shadow form and avoid them entirely! Though, could he? He hadn't yet tried to turn to shadow intentionally. What if it was more difficult that it seemed? And how would he get out of shadow form once he was in it? Justin swallowed his concerns and decided he had to at least try. With lasers still close behind him, he concentrated on turning into shadow!

Justin felt that disintegrating sensation come over his body again. It wasn't as intense as last time, but it was still strong enough for him to let out a soft grunt and close his eyes. When the feeling was gone, he opened his eyes to find that the world had once again turned to colorless outlines. He prayed to the Light that his plan would work.

The soldiers turned the corner and stopped. Justin got some much-needed amusement watching the soldiers' outlines look around in confusion as they wondered where their target went. Eventually, they went back the way they came, and Justin let out a silent sigh of relief.

Justin decided that it would be better to stay in shadow form for the time being to lessen his chances of being spotted again. Besides, if he remembered correctly from last time, he was able to fly in this form, and he figured that would be helpful in getting back to S.o.L. headquarters faster. He had these powers—might as well figure out how they worked.

He took an experimental hop and ended up still falling to the ground. He thought about what this could mean. He got into shadow form by thinking about it; maybe moving in shadow form worked the same way. He thought about moving upward, and sure enough, he felt his feet leave the ground. Having figured out the secret, he took off in the direction of S.o.L. headquarters.

It took longer than he expected as all the landmarks he was familiar with were now black-and-white outlines. Eventually, he resorted to coming back out of shadow form every few minutes in order to regain his bearings. After close to ten minutes of wandering the city, he finally made it back to the rooftop that hid the entrance to S.o.L. headquarters.

Justin came out of shadow form and breathed a deep sigh of relief. "I made it."

CHAPTER 10

Justin entered the building and went all the way down to S.o.L. headquarters. He was tired, he was hungry, his side ached, but even more than that, he wanted to see his home and his friends again. He opened the door and went right on in.

His heart immediately lightened upon seeing fellow S.o.L. agents hang out in the entryway. None of them were any he was personally familiar with; but after almost a whole day of dealing with enemies, it was nice to know that these guys were not going to try and kill him. However, as much as he wanted to just stand there and soak in the feeling of being home, he knew he should report to Director Dusk and let him know of his return as soon as possible. And after that, he wanted to let his team know that he was okay, and he still wanted to find Blake to ask him how to deal with being the Warrior. So, in the hopes of getting all that done as soon as possible, he went off in the direction of Dusk's office.

Just outside of Dusk's office, Justin found his first familiar face. "Hannah!" he called out.

Hannah turned toward Justin and paused as she processed what she was seeing. "Justin?" she said. "Oh my light! It is you!"

She ran up to him and hugged him like a long-lost brother. There was just one problem. "Ribs! *Ribs!*" Justin squealed.

Hannah let go. "Sorry! Forgot you were still recovering," she said.

"It's okay," Justin told her. "It's good to see you too."

"I thought you were locked in the castle dungeon," Hannah pointed out.

"I managed to escape," Justin told her. "I'll explain how later. Right now, I should probably let Director Dusk know I've returned."

"Good idea," Hannah replied. "He's talking with Blake and Martha right now. Just give me a moment."

Hannah knocked on the door and went inside. "Excuse me," she said. "I know you didn't want to be disturbed, but something's come up that you *have* to know about."

Dusk's voice could be heard, clearly annoyed. "What is it?" he asked.

"One of our missing agents has returned," Hannah told them. "Justin's back."

Martha spoke up. "That's impossible," she said. "He was imprisoned in the castle dungeon. There's no way he could have escaped from there."

Justin decided that now would be a good time to make his entrance. "And yet, here I am," he said, entering the room. "Agent 327 finally reporting in."

The three senior members of S.o.L. were taken aback as if they had seen a ghost. Blake was the first to recover. "Justin! Thank the Light you're okay," he said.

"Barely," Justin said. "I had a close call with Imperial soldiers on my way here, and my time in the dungeon wasn't exactly comfortable either, but I should be fine after a little rest."

"But how did you get free in the first place?" Martha asked. "The castle dungeon is supposed to be inescapable."

"I can explain during the debriefing," Justin said. "I know I'm late returning from my mission, but I assume there will still be a debriefing?"

Dusk spoke up. "I think we can arrange something," he said. "However, there are some questions that cannot wait. You were a prisoner of the enemy, however briefly. I need to know if you told them *anything*."

Justin looked Dusk right in the eye. "No, sir," he assured him. "They managed to discover my identity through a DNA test, but that is all they got out of me."

"Were you followed?" Dusk asked.

"No, sir," Justin answered.

"Are you sure?" Dusk asked.

"Positive," Justin said, confident that no one could've followed a shadow. "I made sure to lose all pursuers before entering the area."

Dusk visibly loosened up and breathed a sigh of relief. "That's a relief," he said. "Well done, agent."

"Thank you, sir," Justin said. "Before I go, do you know where my team is? I would like to let them know I'm okay before I do anything else."

"They're currently out on a mission," Dusk told him. "Actually, they're out on your mission."

"My mission?" Justin asked.

Blake explained, "The warehouse reconnaissance mission you and John went on."

This news struck Justin like a bolt of lightning. "WHAT?!" he exclaimed.

"John is dead, and we honestly didn't expect for you to return," Blake continued. "We needed somebody to finish that mission, and since your team wanted to do something to avenge you two, we figured the most feasible way of doing that would be to let them finish what you started."

Dusk spoke up. "We will have your debriefing at the same time as theirs," he said. "You can use the time until then to rest up. You look like you need it."

"No, no, no, you don't understand!" Justin said in a panic. "The warehouse! It's a trap!"

At those words, everyone's expressions suddenly became more worried and anxious.

"A trap?" Dusk asked.

"Yes," Justin replied, still full of worry. "The warehouse is rigged to trap S.o.L. agents inside and placed them in the firing line of a massive weapon they call the Turret Tower. The soldier standing guard outside even has a sensor planted on him to let them know when we've arrived."

Martha spoke up, "This Turret Tower, how dangerous is it?"

"John himself called it the ultimate anti-S.o.L. weapon," Justin said. "It's got multiple cannons, no blind spots, and access to the warehouse's energy supply. The only reason John and I didn't have to face it is because its weapons were offline, but Scorpius said they would be ready by tonight. They will spring the trap on any S.o.L. agents that walk in. Daniel, Molly, and Xavier are practically doomed."

Dusk rushed over to the large computer placed against the back wall. "There may yet be time," he said, pressing a button on the console. "As long as they haven't entered the warehouse yet. This is S.o.L. headquarters calling Pitch! Come in, Agent Pitch! Can you read me?"

Everyone breathed a sigh of relief when Daniel's voice came in over the radio. "This is Agent Pitch," he said. "Forgive me, sir, but I thought we were supposed to maintain radio silence during this mission?"

"Some important new info just came in," Dusk said. "Where are you?"

"We just entered the warehouse," Daniel replied. "We had to take out a guard to get in, but—"

Justin interrupted, "Get out of there! Now!"

Suddenly, a KA-CHUNK was heard over the radio. Dusk spoke into the radio again, a little more panic in his voice, "What's going on? Report."

"A hidden wall just popped out of the ground, blocking the exit!" Daniel said. "We're trapped! Wait! The back wall is lowering… WOAH!"

Laser fire came in loud and clear over the radio.

"Pitch! PITCH!" Dusk cried out.

"It's some kind of tower made of turrets!" Daniel cried out. "It's shooting at us! We have nowhere to go! Requesting backup immediately!"

Dusk was silent for a moment before slamming his fists onto the console in frustration. "Shine it all!" he cursed. "I should've known something was up! Scorpius would not have abandoned something as valuable as neo-plastic unless he had something up his sleeve!"

Martha spoke up. "What do we do, sir?" she asked Dusk.

"What *can* we do?" Dusk pointed out. "If Justin's description is accurate, then none of our usual tactics would be effective against that tower! If we send more agents, we'll just put them in danger as well!"

Hannah stepped forward. "You can't just give up!" she exclaimed. "My friends are in danger! We have to do something!"

Blake turned to Justin. "Justin, is there anything else you can remember about that machine?" he asked. "Anything at all that can help us take it down!"

"I'm thinking," Justin said. "Ugh, if only I had gotten here sooner!" Justin slammed his fists against the wall in a fit of rage!

Meanwhile, everyone else continued to talk strategy. "Maybe we don't bother fighting the tower and just focus on getting the agents out?" Martha suggested.

Dusk shot down that idea. "That tower has multiple turrets. Any avenue of escape we create is only going to become guarded by one of them. Unless we can find some way to take down or distract *all* the turrets, any agent we send in is just going to end up as trapped as Daniel's team."

As the rest debated what to do, Justin continued to lean against the wall in self-loathing. He slowly opened his eyes and looked at his hands. Even though he was wearing gloves, he could still feel the glow of the moon insignia on his right hand. Slowly, an idea came into his head. He took a deep breath and accepted his fate.

"The Warrior," he said.

Everyone became quiet and turned toward him. "What?" Dusk asked, speaking for all of them.

"When John and I were spying on this thing, we did think of one strategy that might work against it," Justin told them. "But it's a plan that only the Warrior can accomplish."

"Well then, we're still out of luck," Dusk said. "John's dead, and we don't know who the next Warrior is."

Martha spoke up, "If there is a next Warrior."

"There is," Justin said. "He's right here."

Justin removed his right-hand glove and showed them the insignia. Everyone stared wide-eyed and slack-jawed as they processed what they were seeing.

Martha was the first to say something. "Is it possible?" she asked, astonished.

Justin simply nodded. "Please, let me go rescue my teammates," he said.

Blake snapped out of his amazement and spoke up. "But Justin," he said. "You're still recovering from your bruised rib, and we can tell that you're currently worn out. Even with the Warrior's powers, going out to fight would put you in serious risk."

"I understand," Justin said. "But sometimes you have to take a risk if you know you can do something to help. Right now, my teammates—my friends—are trapped, and I'm the only one who can save them. The Warrior is supposed to protect others, so please...let me do what I've been called to do."

Dusk, Martha, and Blake looked at each other in silence for a brief moment as they contemplated Justin's words.

Dusk then looked back toward Justin. "Is there anything you need?" he asked.

"Three things," Justin said. "First, I need replacements for all the equipment I lost. Second, I need some way to enter the warehouse—an explosive to blow a hole in the wall or something. Finally, I'm going to need to ask Hannah and Blake for something a little more unique..."

CHAPTER 11

Justin rushed to the warehouse district as quick as he could in shadow form. On the way, all he could think about was how he hoped he would get there before any of his teammates got hurt. Sure, there were literal stacks of neo-plastic they could take cover behind, but even the energy-resistant material would not last forever with four high-powered turrets firing at it. He could not waste a second.

Eventually, he reached the same rooftop he and John were spying from the previous night. He came out of shadow form and located the warehouse his team was currently trapped in. "I've reached the warehouse district," he spoke into his earpiece. "I'm going in."

Dusk's voice came in through the radio. "Understood. Good luck, agent."

Justin jumped down to the ground, turning to shadow to prevent getting injured. Once on the ground, he went back to physical form and ran straight for the target warehouse. Once he got close, he could hear turret fire coming from inside the building, which, surprisingly, comforted him. It meant that at least one of his friends was still alive.

He went to the side of the building and moved toward the back. He picked a spot on the wall which, judging by the sounds, was closer to the tower. He hoped that this would prevent his teammates from getting injured when he blasted a hole in the place. He dug into his utility belt and pulled out the explosive device he was given. He attached it to the wall and activated the timer before running to a safe distance. Once he was clear, he had just enough time to utter a quick, "Dear Light, please let this work."

A BOOM! shook the area! Justin wasted no time running straight to the newly-made hole in the wall! Once inside, he took a quick right, running past the tower and toward a half-melted palette of neo-plastic! He was able to dive behind it just before the turret fire resumed!

As he suspected, that was also where the rest of his team was hiding; and thankfully, all three of them were still okay. "Thank the Light you're okay!" Justin shouted over the turret fire.

All three of them were visibly startled by the re-appearance of their lost friend. "327?!" Molly exclaimed in surprise. "How?!"

"Later!" Justin reminded them. "It's good to see you all too! But right now, we have a Turret Tower to take down!"

Daniel snapped out of his stupor and spoke up. "Right. Right," he said. "So, do you have a plan?"

Everyone huddled closer together so Justin wouldn't have to speak up as much. "I have a plan," he told them. "The problem is that it's a very risky plan, and I can't guarantee it will work."

Xavier voiced his thoughts. "It better not be to just book it to that hole you just made," he said. "The bottom turret is already aimed right at it, waiting for us."

"It's not, but the real plan is not much better," Justin replied. "Basically, we need to turn off the power to this building."

Daniel spoke up. "How do we do that?"

Justin explained the situation. "There's a fuse box on the back wall behind the tower," he told them. "Unfortunately, it's passcode protected, and John and I weren't able to discover what it was—which is why I brought this."

He opened one of the pockets on his utility belt and pulled out a remote-like device that looked like an upgraded version of the one Hannah showed off in the infirmary two weeks prior. Not having been there, Molly asked, "What is that?"

"It's something that Candle's been working on," Justin said, referring to Hannah by codename. "It's meant to disable electronic locks."

"AWESOME!" Molly exclaimed. "What are we waiting for? Let's go ahead and use the thing!"

"I wish it were that easy," Justin told them. "It's still a prototype, and while Candle claims she got it working, thanks to Watcher, it still has a few quirks."

Daniel became cautious upon hearing this news. "Such as?" he asked.

Justin gave them the bad news. "It has to be right up against the lock to work, and the actual unlocking process still takes a while," he said. "Obviously, this will leave me a sitting duck, so while I'm opening the lock, I need you three to distract the tower."

All three of Justin's teammates reeled back at this information, Xavier especially. "You want us to WHAT?!" he asked.

"I told you it was risky," Justin reminded them. "But it's the only plan I've got."

Xavier still wasn't impressed. "Your plan to get us out of danger is to put us in even *more* danger?" he asked incredulously.

"Believe me, I would not ask you to do this if I had any other choice," Justin told them. "But I trust you guys, and I believe you all are capable of surviving until I get the lock open. Once the lights go out, I'll take care of everything. Just distract that tower until then."

His three teammates were silent as they contemplated the risks of this plan. Eventually, Molly spoke up, "Okay! Let's do it!"

Xavier did not share his sister's enthusiasm. "What?! Sis, are you crazy?" he asked. "This plan is going to get us all killed!"

"What would you rather do?" Molly responded. "Sit here until the lasers burn through the neo-plastic? Or maybe run for the hole in the wall to get shot down? If I'm going to die, I'm not going to die like a coward! ATTACK!"

With that war cry, Molly ran out from behind the makeshift barricade and charged at the tower head-on! One of the turrets aimed at her and fired its laser! Molly jumped backward just in time to avoid it! "That all you got?!" she taunted. "A blind man could aim better than any of you Imperial puppets!"

Molly's actions nearly caused her teammates to develop heart attacks. Daniel prepped his shield and called out, "Moth, be careful!" then to Justin, "You trust us, so we'll trust you."

Daniel ran out from behind the barricade, taking out one of his bolas and throwing it at the second turret! The soldier manning the turret got wrapped up and began struggling to try and free himself! The top two turrets instantly began to cover for their teammate and fired at Daniel and Molly! As the two dodged out of the way, Justin and Xavier watched in concern. Xavier gave a deep groan. "This plan of yours better work," he told Justin before running out to help his teammates.

Justin watched as his friends continued to dodge turret fire! With one turret guarding the door, one turret tied up, and the other two turrets dividing their attention between three targets, Justin felt like now would be the best time to move. So, hugging the right wall, he made a run for the fuse box! Once in front of it, he activated the lock-disabler, just like Hannah had shown him, and held it up against the lock! "Come on, Hannah, Blake, don't fail me now," he muttered to himself.

Meanwhile, the other three were still doing their best to distract the turrets! "Come on!" Molly taunted as she dodged a laser. "Did Saul choose the worst cannoneers for this job?! Come on. I dare you to hit me, dummies!"

The soldier manning the top turret seemed to have had enough of Molly's insults. "Keep laughing, you punks!" he called out. "You S.o.L. rats will tire out eventually!"

"Please, I doubt you could even hit me if I was standing still!" Molly shouted back.

As Molly continued to taunt, Xavier rushed forward and struck at the base of the tower with his hammer! The attack did literally nothing, but it caught the attention of the cannoneers, who both fired at Xavier! He dodged the lasers and ran back toward the front of the warehouse!

Daniel took the opportunity to try and throw another bola, but as he tossed it, the top turret noticed and shot the bola out of the air! The laser kept going and was about to hit Daniel, who brought up his shield and braced himself! The high-powered turret blast proved to be too much—the shield shattered, and Daniel was thrown back by the impact! He landed a few feet away with a loud "AUGH!"

Molly stopped her taunting. "PITCH!" she cried out in distress before running to help him!

Daniel was starting to get back up when Molly grabbed his arm and pulled him out of the way of a laser that was aimed at him! This close call angered Xavier, who tossed his hammer at one of the cannoneers! The hammer just barely missed and clanged harmlessly off the tower's armor!

It was at this point that the cannoneer that had been tied up by Daniel's bola managed to free himself! He fired a shot that forced Xavier backward! At the same time, the turret above fired a shot that cut off Molly and Daniel's escape route, forcing the three into a close circle! The top turret leveled straight at them.

"Better give the Light your final prayers, little rats!" the soldier at the top called out. "Ain't nothing gonna save you now!"

At that same time, a small DING! came from the back wall! Justin let out a triumphant "Yes!" before quickly putting away the lock-disabler, opening the fuse box, and flipping the lever inside!

The orange lights on the ceiling suddenly shut off, plunging the room into darkness. The front of the warehouse was pitch black, while the hole-in-the-wall let in just enough moonlight for the back to be barely visible. All three turrets, distracted from their easy targets, swiveled around the tower and aimed at Justin, who faced them with re-awakened confidence. The hard part was now over. It was time to show them what he was truly capable of.

Of course, the soldier at the top didn't know this and began laughing. "You think you're clever, don'tcha?" he called out. "Well, too bad for you, this tower still has an hour's worth of emergency power—which is more than enough time to take care of you rebels!"

"Maybe!" Justin replied. "But I didn't turn off the lights to power you down!"

"Then what for?" the soldier asked, confused.

"To power myself up," Justin said with a grin.

Not even waiting for a response, Justin gave a demonstration and turned to shadow form! The soldiers let out a few exclamations of "Wha?", "How did he?", and "Where did?" before swiveling their turrets all around in an attempt to try and find where he went!

Justin re-appeared on top of the bottom turret, startling the cannoneer, who let out a shriek! Justin quickly struck him with his electric tonfa, paralyzing him! Justin then pried open the control panel on the turret and ripped out a few wires to render it inoperable! The next highest turret noticed what was going on and tried to aim at Justin, but just as he was in its sights, he turned right back to shadow form! A few seconds later, he re-appeared on top of the turret that had aimed at him and repeated the process!

The soldier at the top watched in horror as Justin moved on to the third turret! Just as Justin finished, the soldier decided to bail and began climbing down the tower! About half-way down, he slipped and fell the rest of the way, landing on his back! Justin was ripping out the wires on the top turret, disabling the whole tower as the soldier slowly got back up! He was just starting to race for the hole in the wall when Justin turned to shadow form and re-appeared in front of him! Justin grabbed the soldier and slammed him into the side of the tower! Even with the helmet covering the soldier's eyes, Justin could see he was terrified!

"I-Impossible!" the soldier stuttered. "I was told the Warrior was dead!"

"And you just automatically assumed that there wouldn't be a new one," Justin said with a glare. "I want you to deliver a message to your lord and master, Saul. Tell him about what happened here. Let him know that the Light has chosen a new Warrior to protect his people, and if he asks for a name, let him know it's the agent that just escaped his dungeon: Justin Libra, codename…Shadow."

Justin threw the soldier to the ground, who then picked himself up and ran outside. Justin took off his mask and breathed a sigh of relief. He turned toward his friends and gave them a small smile. They took off their masks to clearly show their shocked expressions.

Soon, however, their slack jaws turned into wide grins. "YEAH!" Molly cried out. "That was awesome!"

Daniel let out a light-hearted chuckle. "I never would've guessed you would be the new Warrior, but I am glad you are," he told Justin. "Thanks for saving us there."

"Hey, I couldn't have done it without you guys," Justin reminded them. "Sorry for placing you in such a dangerous situation."

Xavier went over to pick up his hammer, his face a little more stern than the others. "Eh, we'll forgive you this time," he told Justin. "Just don't forget...we got lucky."

Justin accepted that criticism with a shrug. "I admit it wasn't the best plan ever, but it was the only one I had. So, thank the Light it worked," he said. "Now we better get going before more soldiers arrive."

Molly spoke up, "One more thing—*Shadow*?"

"I know, not a very imaginative codename," Justin admitted. "But I didn't want to use John's old Lunar codename, and it was the best I could come up with on short notice."

"Hey, it's a heck of a lot better than Agent 327," Molly pointed out.

Daniel spoke up, "Agreed, but let's get out of here like Shadow suggested."

Everyone nodded their heads. Justin brought his finger up to his earpiece. "This is Agent Shadow, formerly Agent 327, calling headquarters," he said. "Mission accomplished. Everyone is safe. Returning to base."

With that, they all ran out of the warehouse and returned to S.o.L. HQ.

CHAPTER 12

Justin and his team safely made it back to S.o.L. headquarters. They opened the door to find that almost everyone in the agency was waiting for them. Before Justin could ask what everyone was doing, Hannah came forward, grabbed his right arm, and raised it into the air while removing the glove to show the insignia. "Everyone!" she shouted. "The new Warrior!"

Justin felt his cheeks redden in embarrassment as everyone stared at him in awe. His ears were assaulted as everyone began talking among themselves.

"It really is true."

"So that's the new Warrior."

"Maybe the Light hasn't abandoned us after all," and many other similar comments all fought for attention.

Director Dusk, who was standing front and center, spoke above the noise. "Everyone, quiet down!" he said. "I know it's comforting to see that the Light has chosen a new Warrior, but Agent Shadow and the rest of his team need to rest for their debriefing in an hour. If you wish to get to know him, you can do so later."

As the crowd began to disperse, Dusk turned to Justin's team. "Good job, agents," he said. "I know the mission didn't go as planned, but at least you all returned safely."

Daniel spoke up for his team, "It was close, sir, but we're okay, thanks to Justin."

"Speaking of which," Dusk said, turning to Justin. "I hope you realize this is only the beginning of your work as the Warrior. We will have many missions that require your powers, and you will have to start patrolling the city like the Warriors before you. It will be difficult even with your powers. I hope you are up to the task."

Justin nodded. "I will be…after a bit of rest," he said. "My ribs are still recovering, and honestly, even if they weren't, these past two days have really taken their toll."

"I thought as much," Dusk said. "I've already scheduled another two weeks of rest for you to recover, but after that, the hard work begins."

"Understood, sir," Justin said.

Dusk then addressed the whole team, "Now, as I said before, your debriefing is in an hour. Until then, you are dismissed."

Dusk left, allowing the team to discuss what they were going to do for the next hour. "Well," Xavier said. "I'm going back to my room and taking a nap."

Daniel voiced his opinion. "Not a bad idea," he said. "Just make sure you're awake in time for the debriefing."

"I'll set an alarm. Don't worry," Xavier assured him.

"Just making sure," Daniel replied. "I should probably visit the infirmary. I don't think that turret blast did any serious injury, but it's probably better to check and make sure."

Molly voiced her plans, "In that case, I'll come with you—as long as you don't mind me keeping you company."

"Thanks, Molly. Appreciate it," Daniel said, then turning to Justin, "So, what are you going to do, Justin?"

Justin took a deep breath and thought about it for a second. "I think I'll just hang out on the roof," he said. "I could really use the fresh air."

"Okay," Daniel said. "We'll see you during the debriefing."

With that, everyone went their separate ways. Justin headed back upstairs toward the roof. Once there, he sat on the edge, looking out toward the forest as was his custom. Now that he finally had a quiet moment, he could think back on everything that had happened over the past two days: all the losses, all the close calls, all the questions that he still didn't know the answer to—all of them combined with a realization that life was going to be very different from here on out.

From behind him, he heard the staircase door open and a voice calling out to him. "Mind if I join you?"

Justin looked behind him to see Blake carrying a bundle under his arm. The old man's face caused a small smile to appear on Justin's. "Go ahead," he said.

Blake set the bundle down and sat next to Justin. "I assume you have a lot going through your mind right now," Blake guessed.

"I'm fine," Justin said. "What makes you say that?"

Blake lifted his right hand to show his own white stars insignia. "Justin, it may have been twelve years since I first got this insignia, but I still remember that day clearly," he said. "My mind was so full of questions that I felt like I might go senile. I know you have to be going through something similar."

Justin sighed. "Well, I guess two rather big questions are bugging me," he admitted.

"Well, share them with me, and I'll try my best to help with them," Blake replied.

"First off, why me?" Justin said. "There have to be people much better qualified to protect the city. Why did the Light call me to bear this responsibility?"

Blake nodded in understanding. "That's always the big question, isn't it," he said.

"Let me guess," Justin said. "You had that same question?"

"And so did John when he was chosen," Blake told him. "It seems to be a recurring theme among us Guardians. So, what's your second question?"

"Well, I've been thinking..." Justin said. "If the Light was so quick to choose me as the new Warrior, why has it been nine years and he *still* has not chosen a new Ruler?"

Blake drew in a deep breath. "Tough questions," he said. "And I'm going to be honest with you—I cannot fully answer them yet. I can't read the Light's mind, and he doesn't reveal everything immediately. But I will say this—for nine years, we have been fighting a losing battle. We always believed that the Light had not abandoned us, but for the most part, we didn't have much to justify that faith. That's not to say we had no evidence, but more and more, the rest of the world pushed for a future without the Light. We were but memories of days long past, shadows of a time people trusted the Light. It's where we got the name.

"But now, *you* have happened. In the middle of this Long Night, when the Light has supposedly abandoned his people, he called you to protect them. You are living proof that the Light still cares for us, and that has given us hope again. You saw everyone's faces down there. I may not know why the Light chose you specifically, but I believe we will learn that in time. Until then, find some joy in that hope you bring. Being a Guardian is a big responsibility, and it can sometimes be a burden, but it is also a blessing. Never forget that."

Justin was silent for a second as he took in everything Blake said. Eventually, he spoke up. "Thank you."

"Just doing my job," Blake replied before reaching for the bundle he brought up. "By the way, I also came up to give you this."

Justin took a closer look and realized it was a black scarf. "Is… is this one of John's?" he asked.

Blake nodded. "He wore this scarf to signify that he was the Warrior, give himself some visual distinction from the rest of the agents," he explained. "I'm pretty sure that if he lived to see you carry on his legacy, he would have wanted you to have this."

Justin took the scarf but didn't put it on. In the meantime, Blake got back up and stretched. "Well, I'll let you get some rest," he said. "I'll see you at the debriefing."

With that, Blake went back inside, leaving Justin alone with his thoughts again. Still holding the scarf, he got up and turned to look toward the city—the city he had been called to protect. With a deep breath, he tied the scarf around his neck. As the ends of the scarf blew behind him in the breeze, he made a silent promise. He would rest—for now—but when he returned, he would show the people of Luminous that the Light had not abandoned them. He would protect the city from any threat, whether it be Saul and his henchmen or some random criminal that prowled the streets. This is what the Light called him to do, and he was going to do it.

So swore he, Justin Libra, codename Shadow, the Light's chosen Warrior.

EPILOGUE

Sarah was in her hospital room, still recovering from her broken leg. Recently, she had been allowed to move around a little via crutches, but at the moment she was lying on her bed, strumming her guitar and working out the lyrics to a new song:

No sunrise to spoil the mood!
No one to tell us what to do!
Forget your responsibilities!
Come see what it's like to be free!
We're gonna have fun all night!
Dancing under neon lights!

"Yeah, I like that," she muttered to herself, setting aside her guitar and writing down her new lyrics on her computer's music-writing program.

At that point, she heard the door open and saw her father enter. "Hey, Dad!" she cried out, setting aside her stuff.

Saul was smiling on the outside, but his baggy eyes and slouched shoulders suggested something was wrong. "Hey, Sarah," he said in a groggy voice that only strengthened the impression.

"Dad, are you okay?" Sarah asked.

"Didn't sleep much last night," Saul explained with a yawn. "An important event happened, and we spent all night discussing how we were going to share this information to the public."

"Again?" Sarah asked, surprised. "It was only the night before that the Warrior died. Are you saying something equally as big happened almost immediately afterward?"

"We were surprised as well," Saul said. "I can't tell you all the details at the moment, but basically, a S.o.L. agent sabotaged a major project of ours."

"Okay," Sarah said. "Honestly, I don't see how that's as important as the Warrior's death, but I guess that is confidential?"

"At least until we get more information," Saul told her. "In the meantime, we have placed this agent on our Most Wanted list. He goes by the codename Shadow. So if you ever hear anything about him, let us know. Okay?"

"Shadow," Sarah repeated. "Got it. Is there anything else you know about him? Like what he looks like or who he really is?"

"We have an image of him. It will be shown on the news if you're curious," Saul replied. "His identity…is still unknown. Sorry."

Sarah paused. Was it just her, or did Saul seem to hesitate for a second there? However, she shook that idea out of her head. Her father was tired. It probably just took him a second to check his memory. Either way, it was at this point that Saul's phone started ringing.

"Shine it!" he said. "I have to get back to the castle. Sorry. I didn't mean to spend my entire visit talking about my problems."

"No. No problem," Sarah insisted. "I appreciate any conversation we can have. If it bothers you that much, I've almost finished another song. We can talk about that your whole visit tomorrow—that is, unless *another* important event happens for the third night in a row."

Saul gave a small chuckle. "Let's hope not," he said. "I'll see you tomorrow then. Love you."

"Love you too," Sarah returned.

The two shared a quick hug before Saul left. Sarah then grabbed the television remote and turned the channel to the "morning" news.

She was curious about this Shadow and wanted to see what he looked like. She believed it was a good idea to be as well-informed as possible. She didn't want to randomly see a wanted criminal and *not* be able to tell the authorities about it.

Luckily, the news channel she turned to seemed to be covering the story. "According to reports," a female reporter stated. "Agent Shadow took down four turrets before disabling the Empire's secret project and running off."

Sarah was surprised. Four turrets? By himself? It was suddenly a little clearer just why this Shadow was considered a threat.

The reporter continued. "Security footage is currently being reviewed by the authorities for more clues," she said. "At this point in time, only one image has been released for identification purposes. If you see this man, be sure to notify the authorities immediately."

A zoomed-in picture of the culprit with his mask down appeared on-screen. Sarah immediately paused the video in shock.

It was him—the grey-eyed agent who saved her life during the concert! He was Agent Shadow! But what could this mean?

If Shadow was willing to take out a major Imperial project and get himself placed on the Most Wanted list, then he could not have been as conflicted as Sarah and Saul theorized. But what then? Could someone who was kind enough to save her life willingly work for an organization that was evil? But at the same time, she knew her father and just couldn't believe he was evil either! But it had to be one or the other—either S.o.L. and, by extension, Shadow or her father. Was she just letting the fact Shadow saved her life cloud her judgement? Or was there something about her dad she didn't know about?

No. She had known her father her entire life. Aside from some confidential information that his job didn't let him share, he never kept a secret from her. She had grown up on his ideals and even turned them into songs. She was confident that she knew all she needed to know about her father.

S.o.L., on the other hand, she knew nothing about. She knew they claimed the Light hadn't abandoned humanity and that Saul should be replaced with a Ruler of the Light's choosing, but why did they believe those things? What drove them to do what they do? She lacked that insider's perspective.

Sarah made up her mind. If she was going to find a solution to her dilemma, then she was going to need to look into S.o.L.'s side of the story and see if it held up under scrutiny.

She didn't know how, but she needed to talk to Agent Shadow.

To be continued…

About the Author

Aaron Torrence is a young author living in Central Virginia. He is a Christian and thanks God for the opportunity to share his writing. He started writing fiction when he was a teenager, and his passion for it has only developed further since. In his free time, he likes to read books, take short walks, play video games, and hang out with his family.

Printed in the USA
CPSIA information can be obtained
at www.ICGtesting.com
CBHW020949200224
4502CB00002B/45